THE SKY-CRASHER

SELECTED FICTION WORKS BY L. RON HUBBARD

FANTASY

The Case of the Friendly Corpse
Death's Deputy
Fear
The Ghoul
The Indigestible Triton
Slaves of Sleep & The Masters of Sleep
Typewriter in the Sky
The Ultimate Adventure

SCIENCE FICTION

Battlefield Earth
The Conquest of Space
The End Is Not Yet
Final Blackout
The Kilkenny Cats
The Kingslayer
The Mission Earth Dekalogy*
Ole Doc Methuselah
To the Stars

ADVENTURE

The Hell Job series

WESTERN

Buckskin Brigades
Empty Saddles
Guns of Mark Jardine
Hot Lead Payoff

A full list of L. Ron Hubbard's
novellas and short stories is provided at the back.

*Dekalogy—a group of ten volumes

L. RON HUBBARD

THE
SKY-CRASHER

GALAXY PRESS

Published by
Galaxy Press, LLC
7051 Hollywood Boulevard, Suite 200
Hollywood, CA 90028

Printed in the United States of America.

ISBN-10 1-59212-330-9
ISBN-13 978-1-59212-330-8

Library of Congress Control Number: 2007927541

Contents

Stories from Pulp Fiction's Golden Age

A ND it *was* a golden age.

The 1930s and 1940s were a vibrant, seminal time for a gigantic audience of eager readers, probably the largest per capita audience of readers in American history. The magazine racks were chock-full of publications with ragged trims, garish cover art, cheap brown pulp paper, low cover prices—and the most excitement you could hold in your hands.

"Pulp" magazines, named for their rough-cut, pulpwood paper, were a vehicle for more amazing tales than Scheherazade could have told in a million and one nights. Set apart from higher-class "slick" magazines, printed on fancy glossy paper with quality artwork and superior production values, the pulps were for the "rest of us," adventure story after adventure story for people who liked to *read*. Pulp fiction authors were no-holds-barred entertainers—real storytellers. They were more interested in a thrilling plot twist, a horrific villain or a white-knuckle adventure than they were in lavish prose or convoluted metaphors.

The sheer volume of tales released during this wondrous golden age remains unmatched in any other period of literary history—hundreds of thousands of published stories in over nine hundred different magazines. Some titles lasted only an issue or two; many magazines succumbed to paper shortages during World War II, while others endured for decades yet. Pulp fiction remains as a treasure trove of stories you can read, stories you can love, stories you can remember. The stories were driven by plot and character, with grand heroes, terrible villains, beautiful damsels (often in distress), diabolical plots, amazing places, breathless romances. The readers wanted to be taken beyond the mundane, to live adventures far removed from their ordinary lives—and the pulps rarely failed to deliver.

In that regard, pulp fiction stands in the tradition of all memorable literature. For as history has shown, good stories are much more than fancy prose. William Shakespeare, Charles Dickens, Jules Verne, Alexandre Dumas—many of the greatest literary figures wrote their fiction for the readers, not simply literary colleagues and academic admirers. And writers for pulp magazines were no exception. These publications reached an audience that dwarfed the circulations of today's short story magazines. Issues of the pulps were scooped up and read by over thirty million avid readers each month.

Because pulp fiction writers were often paid no more than a cent a word, they had to become prolific or starve. They also had to write aggressively. As Richard Kyle, publisher and editor of *Argosy*, the first and most long-lived of the pulps, so pointedly explained: "The pulp magazine writers, the best of them, worked for markets that did not write for critics or attempt to satisfy timid advertisers. Not having to answer to anyone other than their readers, they wrote about human beings on the edges of the unknown, in those new lands the future would explore. They wrote for what we would become, not for what we had already been."

Some of the more lasting names that graced the pulps include H. P. Lovecraft, Edgar Rice Burroughs, Robert E. Howard, Max Brand, Louis L'Amour, Elmore Leonard, Dashiell Hammett, Raymond Chandler, Erle Stanley Gardner, John D. MacDonald, Ray Bradbury, Isaac Asimov, Robert Heinlein—and, of course, L. Ron Hubbard.

In a word, he was among the most prolific and popular writers of the era. He was also the most enduring—hence this series—and certainly among the most legendary. It all began only months after he first tried his hand at fiction, with L. Ron Hubbard tales appearing in *Thrilling Adventures, Argosy, Five-Novels Monthly, Detective Fiction Weekly, Top-Notch, Texas Ranger, War Birds, Western Stories,* even *Romantic Range.* He could write on any subject, in any genre, from jungle explorers to deep-sea divers, from G-men and gangsters, cowboys and flying aces to mountain climbers, hard-boiled detectives and spies. But he really began to shine when he turned his talent to science fiction and fantasy of which he authored nearly fifty novels or novelettes to forever change the shape of those genres.

Following in the tradition of such famed authors as Herman Melville, Mark Twain, Jack London and Ernest Hemingway, Ron Hubbard actually lived adventures that his own characters would have admired—as an ethnologist among primitive tribes, as prospector and engineer in hostile climes, as a captain of vessels on four oceans. He even wrote a series of articles for *Argosy,* called "Hell Job," in which he lived and told of the most dangerous professions a man could put his hand to.

Finally, and just for good measure, he was also an accomplished photographer, artist, filmmaker, musician and educator. But he was first and foremost a *writer,* and that's the L. Ron Hubbard we come to know through the pages of this volume.

This library of Stories from the Golden Age presents the best of L. Ron Hubbard's fiction from the heyday of storytelling, the Golden Age of the pulp magazines. In these eighty volumes, readers are treated to a full banquet of 153 stories, a kaleidoscope of tales representing every imaginable genre: science fiction, fantasy, western, mystery, thriller, horror, even romance—action of all kinds and in all places.

Because the pulps themselves were printed on such inexpensive paper with high acid content, issues were not meant to endure. As the years go by, the original issues of every pulp from *Argosy* through *Zeppelin Stories* continue crumbling into brittle, brown dust. This library preserves the L. Ron Hubbard tales from that era, presented with a distinctive look that brings back the nostalgic flavor of those times.

L. Ron Hubbard's Stories from the Golden Age has something for every taste, every reader. These tales will return you to a time when fiction was good clean entertainment and the most fun a kid could have on a rainy afternoon or the best thing an adult could enjoy after a long day at work.

Pick up a volume, and remember what reading is supposed to be all about. Remember curling up with a *great story*.

—Kevin J. Anderson

KEVIN J. ANDERSON *is the author of more than ninety critically acclaimed works of speculative fiction, including The Saga of Seven Suns, the continuation of the Dune Chronicles with Brian Herbert, and his* New York Times *bestselling novelization of L. Ron Hubbard's* Ai! Pedrito!

THE SKY-CRASHER

CHAPTER ONE

No Soap

A very restless, fretful Caution Jones was seated at his desk in the main offices of Trans-Continental Airlines. Outwardly he was very neat and precise. His hair was combed until not one strand varied a millimeter from its rightful place. His white collar was straight-pointed, conservative. His tie was a modest shade—gray. His desk was shining, and papers piled thereon were stacked in neat, square-edged piles, like soldiers drawn up on parade.

Through the large square window he could see a corner of the white, square weather tower which rose from the modernistic field headquarters. He was a hundred feet above the flying field and he could see every detail of its activity. At hand he had every operations detail of the line. In the space of seconds he could have talked with any pilot in the air or on the ground between New York and Los Angeles.

He was a perfect general manager. Reserved, quiet, inspiring confidence and efficiency by his exemplary conduct and his unimpeachable decisions.

But for all his outward appearance, he was writhing down deep in his pilot's heart. He held an inter-office communication which said:

3

From: Office of President
To: J. J. Jones, GM, TCA

Enc. find PO Dept. circular, advising all airlines that Washington is considering a survey of round-the-world mail service, passenger service, express service.

Details have been arranged with foreign countries. Project is to be sponsored by the United States to heighten efficiency.

In view of the many foreign lines operating across this route and in these countries, it will be necessary for the accepted airline to demonstrate superiority over foreign means.

This would require that we dispatch a ship, fully equipped on this flight, that said plane would have to successfully complete the circumnavigation of the globe in order to receive PO Dept. backing. The first man to make this flight carrying mail and perhaps passengers will receive priority over all other lines.

The promised net income would be about one million a year.

Let me have your decision on this as soon as possible.

Craig

PS Think it over good.

Caution was thinking it over with all his wits. A complete airline route around the world. A stupendous undertaking, demanding the highest kind of efficiency. A grueling test. It had been done before, several times, by pilots who went out for the glory of it. Now it might become an everyday commercial reality.

He was reaching for his dictaphone when he saw a line in the PO memorandum:

United States Airlines having already announced its readiness. The time of departure will be set for July 15.

One month away.

Caution scowled. He knew what was expected of him. Craig was having a hard enough time making both ends meet with their ordinary runs. United States Airlines had cut deep into their traffic with cutthroat competition.

It would cost around fifty thousand to make that flight—and TCA couldn't afford to lose that fifty thousand.

Caution saw a silver ship far up in the sky. He saw it Immelmann, loop twice in a row and then start down in a giddy spin as though it would never come out. With a flash of polished wings, it whipped out, did a dangerous slow roll a thousand feet off the ground and started back upstairs, motor yowling.

He started to say, "Good flying," and then with a scowl, he changed it to, "Damned fool! He'll kill himself!" Pam was always doing something like that, blast her. Where was Pam, anyway? He hadn't seen her for three weeks, and they hadn't been together much since that fatal flight early in the spring.

To the dictaphone, "Advise against this flight as being an expensive risk. Commercial circumnavigation is not feasible in present planes. Participation of United States Airlines bars us through added risk. Jones."

He sighed and pushed a buzzer for a stenographer. When

she came and took the cylinder away he almost stopped her. Somehow he felt depressed.

For an instant he allowed himself to dwell upon the sporting possibilities of that flight. It would be a good race—an exciting one. And if they won— He brought himself up by the mental scruff of his neck. Too much of a risk. Impossible.

The silver plane was still cavorting over the edge of the field, barely falling within the Department of Commerce law on stunt flight. The motor changed its pitch like an angry beast snarling. The sun struck fire from the fabric and the prop. That pilot was having a good time.

"But that sort of thing doesn't get aviation anywhere," muttered Caution.

He thought about that for a while. Safe and sane flying advanced flight, stunts retarded it. Aviation was a business, coming out of swaddling clothes. Pilots were no longer half devil, half eagle. They were responsible men who had serious work to do. Aviation was as dangerous as you made it, and until the public stopped thinking that aviation *was* dangerous, airlines would still show their earnings on the red side of the ledger.

Stunts never got anybody any place. Caution said it with a determined clamp of his jaw. This round-the-world service would almost fall under the heading of a stunt.

On his wall he had long ago tacked a chart. It was more decoration than anything else. Done in small galleons and spouting whales, with palms where Africa was outlined and with Pizarro down with the Incas, and with cherubs, blowing with puffed-out cheeks, showing the prevailing wind directions. Yes, the chart was very ornamental. It showed the routes of Columbus, the more deserving Vasco de Gama, of Magellan. . . .

Caution stood before the chart with his hands behind his back. Magellan's route was traced in dotted lines.

What an undertaking that had been! It had taken from the tenth of August, 1519, until late fall, 1522—a lapse of three years. One thousand days and more. Magellan dead in the Philippines, his ships wrecked and abandoned, his crew dying from scurvy and starvation and thirst, killed by savages, buffeted by mighty storms.

Magellan had accomplished the dream of Columbus, had never lived to see that one vessel, the *Victoria*, limp into port at Spain.

And now they were going to do it regularly, in one week's time.

His nostrils quivered a little. He saw the names on the chart: The Aleutians, Japan, Russia, Poland, Germany and France. Angrily he turned away from the map and threw himself into his desk chair.

Craig, hair bushy and stiff as steel wool, his face the color of raw beef, entered with a militant stride and thumped himself onto the edge of the desk.

"What's this note you sent me?" demanded Craig. "You don't like this world flight?"

"No," said Caution. "That's what I'm paid to do."

"What?"

"See that TCA keeps going."

"But look at that potential earning!"

"United States Airlines," said Caution, with a shake of his head, "is going in for this thing. And they're after our scalps. They're buying up our stocks, cutting our rates and shortening our schedules. Mercer is going to hammer us into the middle of next week. And if Mercer and United States Airlines don't want us in that race, they'll see that we stay out, or kill our pilot."

"Nuts!" said Craig.

"And," said Caution, "we're almost on the rocks. We can barely keep running."

Craig sat up, astonished, blowing hard. "Why didn't you tell me?"

"My job is to keep you from working hard, isn't it? You have enough to worry you. But you can look at our ledgers. We're running in the red, and if things don't pick up, TCA will disappear from the skyways. All the work you and I have done will be gone. Wrecked. We're lucky to be going at all. We need every pilot to keep us in the air. We need every penny to keep the planes in the air. We *can't* afford to make that flight."

"Who said so?"

Caution looked very official, very earnest. "United States Airlines is trying to push us out. If we enter this race—call it yellow if you want—we'll lose out. We don't play the game crooked, and they do."

Craig took the wrapper off a cigar and then began to gnaw upon it as a dog gnaws a bone. He considered Caution for several seconds, speculation in his eye.

"Caution," said Craig, "if I didn't know you better, I'd say you *were* yellow."

Caution took it without a blink. "You pay me to say these things and do these things, not to stunt and romp around like a colt."

"Sure, sure, I know. But listen here, Caution, I've always wondered just what the hell was wrong with you. Now don't get me wrong. You're a crack pilot and you've got a fine business head. But what's under all this?"

Caution's lean face changed. His mouth drew down on one side, his left eye closed ever so little. The expression completely transformed him. It was bitter, reckless. Craig was startled. He had never seen Caution look that way before.

"You want to know the truth?" said Caution. "My dad was Batty Jones. Did you know that?"

"Why—why, yes, I'd heard of it. He was a famous circus pilot, wasn't he?" the TCA man asked.

"Yes," said Caution, biting off the word. "A famous circus pilot, nothing more. They called him Batty. He *was* batty. He grew up out of the war. He didn't give a damn for anything, not even my mother's feelings or my future. He was a *stunt* pilot.

"He starred with the old Bates Flying Circus, the craziest fools aviation ever bred. He came out of the JN-9 era and flew himself up into the money and fame. He was the idol of all kids. He didn't have a nerve in his body. He looked like me, but that's where the resemblance ended.

"One time, off Florida, he flew down a twenty-foot alley

9

with a plane which spread its wings forty feet. One time he wrecked ships, diving them straight in from thousands of feet, just to give the crowd a thrill. One time he arranged with a pilot so that they'd smash their ships together in midair just to amuse the mob. They did it, and the other pilot died. Batty Jones got out with a busted arm and a scratched ear.

"His stunts were famous. Anything for a stunt. Anything for a thrill. He lived hard and high and fast. He was the best pilot in the world, and he turned that talent into money by amusing people, by giving them chills. He was a *stunt* pilot, get me?"

Craig sat very still, amazed at Caution's wild tone. Caution got up and paced down the room, scowling, eye squinted, mouth drawn bitterly down.

"He wouldn't fly sanely. He wouldn't give aviation a break. No, he dangled off wings, looped ships ready to fall apart, parachuted, cracked up, burned in the air and came out of it every time, grinning.

"A circus pilot. They didn't last long. In 1928 my dad burned the ship in the air, figuring that he could bail out in his chute. A wing hit him when it folded. I watched him burn a thousand feet above the earth. I thought it was just another stunt until I . . . until they . . .

"My mother was worn out with it. The final shock killed her. I greased ships, stole rides, stole time, licked boots, begged an education in the air. And I ordered myself to keep sane and steady. I had to do it, and I've done it. I'm 'Caution' Jones, the levelest head in the business."

As though suddenly tired, he sat down. When he lit a cigarette, Craig saw that his hand was shaking. He'd never seen Caution like that before.

"Then," said Craig, after a long pause, "I guess we don't want to try that round-the-world flight. You're right, Caution, it's a stunt. No reason to do it. But still—we've got to get out of this hole somehow. I've put my life into TCA, you've given it years yourself. It's all we've got. And we don't want to take a beating lying down just because a gang of crooks like United States Airlines tries to muscle in on it.

"However, we'll find something else, something less spectacular. The round-the-world flight is out."

Unseen by both, the silver ship which had lately been stunting over the field had landed. A slim, booted figure had stepped out, and now that person was standing in the doorway, looking at them.

"What's this about a round-the-world flight?" said Pam Craig, swinging her helmet and goggles back and forth. Her blonde hair was rumpled, her eyes were alight with the joy of living, her mouth was drawn into a reckless smile.

"Pam!" said Craig.

"Where did you come from?" demanded Caution.

"Didn't you see my show?" said Pam, a little grieved. "I did everything but smear in, and you didn't even notice. That isn't very complimentary to my flying!"

"Your stunting," corrected Caution.

"My flying," corrected Pam.

"Where have you been?" said Craig.

"Down to Florida. I had the best time! The air races were simply marvelous. But I didn't place. I wrecked my landing gear the first day and couldn't enter."

"Florida?" said Caution. "That's high-speed stuff!"

"Well, look at my plane!" invited Pam.

The two men glanced out the window and saw the silver wings crouched before the hangar. The ship was mostly motor, built for speed, a small, wicked crate, hard to handle, capable of six miles a minute.

"Where did you get that?" Craig barked.

"Bought it," said Pam, seating herself on the desk. She cleared away the orderly papers by simply knocking them off with her hand. Caution, the soul of neatness, growled deep in his throat.

"You'll spend every cent you've got," said Craig.

"My mother left it for me to spend, didn't she? And besides, I've still got seventy-five thousand dollars, and when that's gone, TCA will have a job for me. You'll make me a line pilot—and I'll be so famous you'll have to pay me seven hundred a month."

Her silver-gray eyes were filled with audacity. She was small, about five feet two, but her enthusiastic, vibrant bearing seemed to give her height.

Craig snorted. "What good would *you* be as a line pilot?"

Caution nodded sagely. "What would we want of a stunter on this line? You'd better save your money, Pam."

"You'd better save your advice, Mister Caution. Now what's this I hear of a round-the-world flight in which we're taking part?"

"We're not taking part," said Craig. "It's too much of a risk. We're staying home this time."

Pam looked downcast about it. "You mean—you mean you'll let United States Airlines walk away with it?"

Caution was very uncomfortable. "We're not letting anyone do anything, Pam. It's too much of a risk. The flight will cost over fifty thousand, without including the possible loss of the plane. We simply can't take the loss, that's all."

Pam started out, very thoughtful, lower lip caught in her teeth.

Caution watched her go with a queer sensation in his throat. She was beautiful, gay, reckless, completely demoralizing, and if he would only admit it, he admired and respected her.

"Stunt pilot!" said Caution Jones as scornfully as he could, and went back to his work.

CHAPTER TWO

"WE CAN'T GET OUT OF IT!"

A T ten o'clock the next morning, Caution, working hard at his desk, scowling as he read bad passenger reports, heard the approach of a strange ship. It was not one of the line, he knew, and he looked out through the great square window to see a scarlet plane, two-motored, speedy and painted with the eagle emblem of United States Airlines.

"Mercer's private ship!" thought Caution in surprise, and immediately called Craig to apprise him of the fact.

"Come on in here," said Craig. "I may have need of a strong man."

Caution watched Mercer alight on the runway. Mercer was hard of face, tall, dressed in flashy clothes. He was followed by a man Caution knew to be Ewell, chief pilot of Mercer's line, and another man, MacTaggart, who was Mercer's private pilot.

The trio, walking with a swagger, looked about at the TCA field with disdainful and amused eyes. MacTaggart was commenting on the place in a loud tone of voice, wagging his overlarge head, which sat like a pumpkin on his small, gangly body. Ewell, a blustering brute with a thick jaw, long arms and a bull neck, laughed uproariously.

Caution rattled a pencil thoughtfully against his white even teeth and then went down the steps that led to Craig's office. He had been there but a moment when the three entered—without knocking.

Craig remained seated at his desk. Caution took a position against the wall. Mercer, with his two henchmen on either side, slammed the door shut so hard that the glass rattled.

"Well?" said Mercer, giving his light felt hat a tug down over one slitted eye.

"Well, what?" said Craig.

"Are you or are you not entering the round-the-world flight?"

"And if I am?" said Craig, his face impassive, but growing red with anger.

Mercer growled and looked down at his heel, which he turned with a grinding motion. "Then I'll squash you like that, see? I'm tired of monkeying around with a dinky outfit like TCA. I'm tired of playing with you. And I'm not going to let you muscle in on this race."

"No?" said Craig.

"No." Mercer advanced, laid his hands, palm down, on Craig's desk, thrusting his jaw within an inch of Craig's face. "Are you or are you not?"

Craig's steel-wool hair was rising like the hackles on a dog's back. Very deliberately he stood up, shaking with rage. "Get the hell out of here!" he stormed.

Ewell and MacTaggart sidled up closer, paying no attention to Caution whatever.

"I'll enter that race," cried Craig. "I'm sending in my entry blank this afternoon—this morning—right now! No two-for-a-cent apes like you can come in here and tell me what to do. Now get out!"

Mercer stepped back and jerked his thumb at Craig. "After him, boys. I see we'll have to get rough."

Ewell flexed his arms to loosen them in his sleeves. He reached out confidently, almost touching Craig's collar with his small hand.

Suddenly something hit Ewell's shoulder. He whirled about. Caution released his grip and drew back his fist as though he carried a pile driver in it. Ewell started to dodge. He had seen Caution before, had never paid any attention to him. Now he saw that Caution's eye was narrow, that Caution's mouth was dragged down at one corner.

Caution struck. The blow sounded like a thump of a bass drum. Ewell went spinning back, upending a chair, falling into the corner.

With a yowl, MacTaggart threw himself upon Caution. Caution, unruffled, picked him up, held him at arm's length and shook him the way a Newfoundland shakes a terrier. He dropped MacTaggart as one drops something unclean.

Mercer roared, "What the hell you trying to do?" It had all happened so fast that he had not yet realized where things stood. He made an unfortunate move toward his hip pocket. Caution grabbed the wrist, jerked it up, and the gun Mercer had had went spinning down the rug. Then Caution carefully measured the distance to Mercer's nose and let drive.

With a shrill yelp of pain, Mercer folded up. But Caution did not let him drop, Caution struck again. His narrowed eye was seen by Mercer through a reddening blur. Mercer yelled with terror and tried to strike back, but Caution was doing the hitting just then.

17

Caution struck. The blow sounded like a thump of a bass drum.
Ewell went spinning back, upending a chair,
falling into the corner.

At Caution's third blow, Mercer went backward like a catapulted stone. His back struck the door. Glass shattered about his head. He slammed out into the corridor and lay there, quite unconscious.

Caution's voice was shaking. "Now, you yellow pups, get out of here! Pick that guy up and take off, get me? Take off!"

Ewell, sullen and bruised, slunk out. MacTaggart, sidling away from Caution, helped Ewell pick up Mercer. The three were gone. A moment later the roar of the departing plane beat down upon the field.

"Good boy!" applauded Craig, still behind the desk. He had been unable to help, unable to get around his desk in time.

Caution, dusting off his hands and straightening his tie, said, "Like hell I'm 'good boy.' I'm a fool, and so are you. You know what will happen now. They were after our hide before. They'll make certain of it now."

It was then that Craig remembered that he had said he would enter the race. "Oh, gosh!" he groaned. "We'll never make it now—never! And I can't back out."

"No, not now," said Caution. "We'll have to go through with it."

"You make the flight," pleaded Craig.

"All right, I'll make the flight. But it's a stunt flight."

"You've surveyed routes for us. You're the best navigator in the game. You'll get through."

"I doubt it," said Caution. "What'll I use for a plane? And money? Lord knows we haven't got any!"

"Take a regular transport," said Craig.

"For a twenty-thousand-mile hop? You're crazy!"

"You'll have to. Go on, Caution, you can do it. You can do anything."

Caution sighed, and turned to leave. He stopped as though held back by a mighty hand.

Pam was framed in the shattered door, swinging helmet and goggles, ready for a flight to some unknown destination. Pam was laughing, lightly, mockingly.

"Good old Caution!" said Pam. "You should have been a prizefighter!"

"That was a silly thing to do," said Caution.

"Silly, but interesting," said Pam. "When do we start?"

"We?"

"I'm going with you, of course. Unless I make a flight like that, my old man won't give me a line-pilot rating. Let's get busy, Caution!"

Caution felt his heart leap inside him, but he remained calm. "We shall see about that, Miss Craig. We shall see!"

CHAPTER THREE

FLAMES WRECK THE HOP

THE transport plane was a wobbly winged affair, coughing in all three motors, shabby of cabin, sloppy on the controls. But, as Caution remarked to himself, TCA couldn't afford to take a plane off the run, and you didn't fly around the world without something in which to fly.

He stood in the afternoon sunlight and despairingly eyed the ship. It had been decaying for a year in the back of the hangar, unfit for passenger service, unable to obtain a D of C rating. Now, with a large, experimental X painted upon its mud-colored side, it was waiting for the test flight.

Craig, running nervous fingers through his steel-wool hair, said, "It will have to do, Caution. The mechs have been working on it for about three days and they've done all they can do. Damn it, Caution, I didn't know we were so low on funds!"

Caution sighed like a martyr. Pam was coming across the tarmac.

"She's a wreck," said Pam. "That'll have to do some flying to get around the world. What's it fly on, its reputation?"

"I guess so," said Caution.

"You aren't living up to your name," said Pam.

"I know it, but what can I do about it? Absolutely nothing!"

"Seen anything of Ewell, MacTaggart or Mercer?"

"No. I guess they're scared off."

Pam looked surprised. "That's funny! I just saw Ewell walking down the highway toward town. I thought he must have been up here to see you."

"Wasn't around here." Caution waved to a mechanic. "Start her up!"

The motors came to life, protesting mildly, as though such long faithful service deserved better fate. Caution swung in under the control column, preparatory to starting off. He was aware of Pam. She was settling herself in the cabin behind him.

"Lay off!" said Caution. "I don't know what this boat will do!"

"I'm coming along anyway," said Pam, unruffled. "I'm curious to see how this antique rides."

Disgustedly, Caution climbed down and came back a moment later dragging a pair of seat pack chutes, which he heaved into the cabin. Then, with a righteous air, he started the plane rolling down the runway, into the wind.

The motors bellowed in jarring discord, the wings shook, the wheels stayed logily on the concrete.

Pam looked worried.

"She'll never take off with a full load," muttered Caution.

It seemed that the ship would never rise. Yard by yard the runway flew by. Pam began to sit up, staring at a long fence which blocked the far end of the runway. Caution sawed at the controls, back and forth, back and forth, as though he could make the plane take off by physical strength alone.

Suddenly the rumbling stopped. They staggered through the air, faltering, unable to climb except slowly.

Pam nodded to herself as though satisfied that her guess was right.

"Is it true that TCA is broke?" said Pam.

Caution nodded. "But that isn't for publication. United States Airlines have us right where they want us."

Sluggishly they made their way up to five thousand feet. The din of the clattering engines was deafening even in the ancient soundproof cabins—but Caution's keen ears detected something else.

"Sound funny to you?" he said to Pam.

"Kind of."

"Sounds more than funny to me. What do you suppose is wrong?"

Pam looked at the gas gages and saw them registering full. She looked at the oil and then, pointing at the meter, she said, "Slipping down."

The oil pressure was going, not fast, but going just the same. The gas gages were flickering. Oil temperature began to creep up, its white needle like the bony finger of a skeleton. And then Caution understood. He pulled all three throttles to him with a savage jerk. The roar of the engines died. In the comparative silence of whistling struts, a low hissing sound made itself known.

"Sugar in the gas," said Caution. "It cakes the carbon, shuts off the oil, fills the crankcase full of gas. Hold tight while I dead-stick it in."

They both heard a low cough from the starboard motor,

they both smelled the ugly odor of smoke. Pam's eyes grew rounder. The plane was falling off on one wing. The ground below looked topsy-turvy, very far away and very hard.

Tongues of flame began to lick back. The gas in the hot crankcase, ignited by sparks from the working parts, had exploded. In an instant, the whole trailing edge was burning, sending back thin streamers of gray smoke.

Caution stood up, leaving the controls. It was already growing hot in the cabin. Mutely, he pointed to one chute and picked up the other.

The lurching cabin was grayed until they could scarcely see each other. Pam's hands were shaking. Caution's eye was narrow, his mouth drooping on one side. Strapping on his chute, Caution held open the cabin door.

"Jump," said Caution.

Pam looked at that faraway ground. She started to step back. It wasn't her first jump, but it always affected her that way. She felt a strong hand on her shoulder. A mighty push sent her out into space. She fell away from Caution like a dropped bomb, turning over and over, growing smaller and smaller.

Caution stepped out. He was not worrying about his chute. A jumper never does. He was worrying about Pam. Would she land in a tangle of shrouds and break a limb? Would she land in the clear?

Air whipped upward into his nostrils. His chest seemed to inflate. He felt empty and inanimate. He pulled his rip cord, saw the white pilot chute blossom over his head, saw the bigger silk come streaking out to whip open. The jar of the harness against his arms jerked him right side up. He looked down at the swinging world. Everything was spinning. He still had a thousand feet to fall through.

The world was opening up under him like the jaws of a trap. He knew the spot where he would land. That was stationary. Everything else was drawing away from him, as though making a hole for his landing place.

It was a queer sensation, seeing the earth move, grow concave, get bigger under him. Pam was drifting close to the ground, about to land. He saw her chute collapse as though smashed down by an invisible palm.

Doubling up he waited for the earth to smite him. He was aware of a roaring sound above him. He saw the ship coming down, blazing across the skies, leaving a greasy trail of smoke. Even as he looked, a gas tank went. Motors and wings parted company. The fuselage, a lumpy javelin, shot past him and landed, breaking into fresh flames.

He hit hard, doubled up and bounced to his feet to spill his chute. Pam was standing a few yards away, her arms full of white silk, laughing at him.

"You will push a lady!" she said.

"You got out, didn't you?"

"Yes, I got out, my hero. But that's the end of your world flight, isn't it?"

Caution remembered that it was. He sighed wearily. United States Airlines would laugh him out of the sky.

"If it is," said Pam, "then I'll begin my world flight."

"*Your* world flight?"

"Sure. I've got the plane already picked out, the cashier's check in my pocket, the entry blank registered with the PO Department."

"Well—well, for ever more!" said Caution.

CHAPTER FOUR

TRAINED ROBOT?

TWO weeks later, Caution received a telegram from Washington. Craig, suspecting that the worst was about to happen, walked up and down the rug while Caution read the message:

PLANE READY STOPPING POINTS PREPARED
PLEASE MEET ME AT WASHINGTON AIRPORT
THIS AFTERNOON THREE O'CLOCK PLANE
AS I HAVE ENGAGEMENT WITH PO DEPT
CONCERNING MAIL

Caution stood up, put on his hat and extended his hand to Craig. "Well," said Caution, "I'll be seeing you sometime."

"What's up?"

"Pam bought a ship, she's all ready to go. I'm going down to help her settle up the last details of the flight."

"Pam—Pam bought a ship!" stammered Craig. "What do you mean? For what?"

"For the world flight. She's seeing you through with her last cent."

"I won't have it!" cried Craig. "That scatterbrained idiot can't do it—I won't let her! By hell, I've got *some* control over her. Caution, you tell her to sell—"

"She's ready to pull you out of a bad spot," said Caution.

"And because you made that brag to Mercer, I'll have to help out."

"You said yourself she's a stunt pilot. What's the idea, Caution? You've got to stop it, I tell you!"

But Caution was already gone, sorrowful, but resigned.

He alighted at Washington Airport and met a very vivacious, very beautiful Pam. Her eyes were merry, her lips laughing. She was dressed in a filmy print dress, which was set off by a large picture hat.

"Caution himself!" said Pam. "Did you bring your hot water bottle and everything?"

"Where's the ship?" growled Caution.

"Down the road, at the visitors' port. I bought it right here from a fellow who lost heart at the last moment. It only cost seventy-five thousand dollars, Caution."

He blinked. "But that's all the money you have left!"

"What of it? We'll win this race." She immediately dismissed all chances of their failing to win with a wave of her hand. "Wait until you see this crate, Caution—but don't you call it a crate, it's a beauty. Fitted out with extra tanks, leather seats. It's a flying apartment. Parlor, bedroom and sink. Come along!"

Caution, following her down the road toward the other hangar, could not help but smile in admiration of both her beauty and her resource. He felt proud of her, though he did not quite know why.

In the hangar, Caution saw the shadow of great wings. Pam stood like a ringmaster outside and presented him to her craft.

"Looks solid," said Caution, entering to inspect it better.

Pam explained, "Twelve hundred horse power. Flies a payload of two thousand one hundred pounds, climbs a thousand feet a minute, supercharged for altitude flying. I've had tanks built in, and her cruising range as she is—and get this, Caution—her cruising range is four thousand five hundred miles, loaded with that extra ton of gas."

"Uh-huh," said Caution. "But does it fly?"

"Fly!" cried Pam, excitedly, her cheeks glowing, her eyes throwing off sparks. "Just look at her lines! Look at her motors! And you ask me if it flies. Some day, Caution Jones, I'm going to lose patience with you!"

"We'll test it in the morning with a full gas load," said Caution. "We'd better be getting up to the PO—"

A shadow fell between them and the light. Two shadows.

A grating voice said, "Looks just like an airyplane, by golly!"

MacTaggart.

"Might even fly, if it had any pilots around," agreed the companion.

Ewell.

Caution looked slowly at Pam. "You run along. I'll just stay here."

Pam, her eyes a little afraid, edged out of the hangar and hailed a cab.

Ewell and MacTaggart came closer to Caution, smiling. "No hard feelings," said Ewell.

"Hope not," chimed MacTaggart, his oversized head wobbling perilously above his small body.

Caution eyed them with great distaste. "No, no hard feelings."

"Then I guess," said the hulking Ewell, "that we'd better

29

talk to you a little. That is, if you don't mind." He sent an elephantine wink toward MacTaggart.

They came very near before Caution set down his traveling bag. "You gentlemen always seem to be going off half-cocked," he said.

Ewell thrust out his jaw, flexing his arms and clenching his fists, anxious to get this job over with. With Caution in a hospital—

MacTaggart reached inside his belt band and drew out a monkey wrench, which seemed to be his standard weapon of defense.

"Yes," said Caution smoothly, "you always act before you think—and now it's gotten you into trouble."

MacTaggart frowned.

"He's thinking of the coppers," said Ewell.

"No," said Caution, almost languidly. He dipped his hand into his coat and suddenly the two were confronted with a gun muzzle that looked as large as a train tunnel. It was not exactly trained at them, nor was it exactly turned away.

"I thought I'd take a precaution this time," said Caution. And before either of them could move he started shooting. Ewell screamed as though he was mortally hit. MacTaggart found his legs and used them. Spurts of dust, driven upward by smashing lead, flicked about four ankles. The two departed, leaving the monkey wrench behind. Caution placed another clip in the automatic and thrust it back into his pocket. When the startled mechanic came in to investigate the reason for the noise, he found Caution puttering with the inertia starter of the right engine.

Ewell screamed as though he was mortally hit.
MacTaggart found his legs and used them.

"It backfires something terrible," said Caution.

Pam came back at dark, bringing a stalwart pair of gentlemen she "found in an office," and Caution consented to leave the plane for the night.

The next two days were filled with quick activity. Other ships had been heard from up and down the coast. Other companies and even free-lance pilots were willing to take a shot at a contract which might possibly net a million a year.

Caution listened to these reports quietly, as though he had no great part in it, but when Pam secretly watched him, she saw that his eyes were overbright and that his hands shook from excitement.

"He's coming around," said Pam to herself.

There was not much time in which to prepare a flight on so grand a scale, but there had been others who had gone before, blazing the trail, establishing fuel bases about the globe, and it was only necessary to send a wire here, a radio there, to get everything in order.

The papers were at work, playing up the flight, making it a stunting proposition, much to Caution's disgust. He was intensely glad when they were able to take off one morning for New York, the starting point.

The big ship flew easily. Equipped with that gadget every pilot calls a "rabbit," it did not require a pilot constantly at the controls. The gyroscopic robot pilot flew better than a human pilot, if anything. However, due to such matters as precession, the automaton had to be adjusted every five minutes by the clock.

Craig did not come out to see them in New York. Pam mournfully accepted his absence.

"I'm just a worry to him, that's all," she confided to Caution, sitting in the ship at dusk. "I'll never be anything but a girl."

Caution laughed. "Biological truth, Pam. But why regret it? I think you—" He stopped a moment, swallowed. "I think you make a very nice girl," he finished.

"Caution Jones, if I didn't know you better I'd think that that was a compliment!"

"Huh!" said Caution.

She reverted to her despondent mood. "No, he'll never think I'm anything but a bothersome little child in pigtails. I wish he had come out."

"Probably doesn't trust himself."

"I guess so. You know, Caution, this might—might be the last time he sees me. There's the Atlantic, and Europe and Asia, and then—worst of all—the Pacific. And, worse than any of them, United States Airlines."

"You like him, don't you?"

"I think he's the best ever, Caution. But he wanted a boy. He wanted someone to take over all his holdings, and he's said a dozen times in the past couple years that he had no one to take his work after him. I did so want to please him, but all he does is bawl me out. It's been hard to bear. But here, here, I'll be crying the first thing you know, and Pam Craig never cries. She's a very tough customer, Caution, that Pam Craig."

For a long time she was silent, barely visible in the dusk.

"He—he thinks more of you than he does of me. You're his trained robot. . . . Oh, Caution, I'm sorry! I didn't mean—"

Caution had brought himself forward in the pilot's seat. "His what? Tell me straight, Pam; that isn't what they think of me, is it?"

"No. No, Caution, of course not."

Trained robot, thought Caution. Was it possible that they missed the necessity for—? Trained robot. . . .

CHAPTER FIVE

THE ATLANTIC ROLLS BELOW

TANKS brimming, wings burnished, the plane was ready at four o'clock that morning, ready to swoop upward into the graying sky and soar into the east, across the Atlantic, across Europe, Russia, Japan, the Pacific and then North America.

Pam, shivering in the morning chill, stood close to Caution. "You admit it's ready? My lord, Caution, you're slipping! You really mean there's nothing wrong? You mean we're actually in fine shape, ready to take off?"

Caution, with a smile, nodded. "Maybe I'd better look at the engines again, though. I—"

A field official came up. "The USA crowd is away. They left ten minutes ago. Spanner is not at his port. Must have taken off in the night. You'd better get gone, Mr. Jones."

"They didn't wait for dawn, the chiselers!" said Pam.

"First dog there is the first dog hanged," said Caution.

The cabin of the ship was roomy, aglitter with instruments. Caution slid under the controls, jammed both boosters down. The engines started with a growing whine, already warm.

Pam, shivering still, but no longer cold, slid down beside him. "He didn't come out to the field," muttered Pam.

Caution wasn't listening to her. He had the ancient battle

on his hands, getting on. But this time the runway was dry, the wind was crisp and right. A good omen for the flight.

He headed the big black plane into the wind and tested her engines with the brakes on. His jaw was working steadily, his eyes were narrow with calculation. The left was squinted a little, his mouth was down on one side. Pam, startled at his expression, forgot their danger for a moment and stared at him. She had never seen Caution look like that. Somehow, the intensity of his gaze on that runway made her shiver, but not from either cold or excitement this time.

The brakes went off. The plane shook in every rib. The runway was suddenly blurred. Pam held her breath. They skittered across the concrete, grinding, grinding, grinding. Their landing gear lightened slightly, a little more and the wings were biting air.

They were off.

How easy it had been! Pam felt that something was different with the ship. Something was changed, but she could not quite place it.

Caution streaked level for an instant and then whipped the mighty plane into a charging bank, almost ninety degrees, away from the wind, into the east. Under his sure hands, the course was corrected in a moment. Less than a hundred feet off the ground, they headed straight out into the glowing red radiance of the coming sun, heading east, and east again.

Pam was suddenly sure of herself. The thought which had plagued her for years was back with her again, but she felt certain that this time she would put the problem aside forever.

Caution streaked level for an instant and then whipped the mighty plane into a charging bank, almost ninety degrees, away from the wind, into the east.

After this, Craig would have to admit that she could fly, that she was an asset to the Trans-Continental Airlines.

Caution was thinking a thought of his own.

They reached the sea before the world came bright about them. They plunged above the wave crests, flying low for the added speed. Their spreading wings made dark shadows flit through the water.

Land was gone behind them. Not even a steamer was in sight. They were all alone, flying at a speed of two hundred miles an hour above the sea. This same sea had taken other flyers. And some had not come back.

Caution was thinking, "Trained robot!"

Pam was thinking, "Maybe if I'm successful this time—"

Caution's left eye was slightly lowered, his mouth drooped a little—the expression of the daredevil since mankind had been begun. If his father could have seen him he would have smiled knowingly.

But habit is strong. Caution, at the end of the first swift hour, said, "This rabbit doesn't seem to be working right. A little heavy on the right wing. Guess we'd better fly her by hand. A lot safer."

Pam smiled into the din of straining wings and shrieking steel. Below, the Atlantic licked fitfully at their smooth hulk, as though remembering the times when it had proved stronger than men or ships, or than winged planes flying. . . .

CHAPTER SIX

RUSSIAN BAYONETS

L ATE that afternoon, when they had been some twelve hours on their thundering way, Caution unlimbered their two-way radio set and tuned it in while Pam flew. Caution was calm, composed and confident. They were more than halfway across and he could call both sides with the radiophone.

For ten minutes, he sent out his call and was then answered by his home field in New York. The call went through, thanks to the courtesy of the telephone company, and in a moment he was talking to Craig.

"Hello, Caution," said Craig, almost inaudible through the static crackles.

"Hello," said Caution. "Fine weather, everything going fine. We'd be out of range in a few hours and I thought I'd better set your mind at ease. The ship flies like a honey."

"Caution," said Craig, "it's lucky—lucky you started out like that. I've just found out something which—which— Listen, Caution. United States Airlines is buying up TCA stock. There's a rumor going the rounds that we're—"

"I understand," said Caution, "but remember, the world's listening to this. We'll make this flight all right. Hold out for a week, then we'll be home."

"Okay," said Craig despondently.

"Okay," said Caution.

"Did he say anything about me?" said Pam.

Caution, starting to hang up, said, "Sure. Told me to tell you to take care of yourself."

She nodded, but she did not believe him.

The buzzer rasped and Caution put the headphones on again. A voice so loud and clear that it almost deafened him came through. MacTaggart.

"Hello, little boy," said MacTaggart. "What does your octant say?"

"That we're a degree ahead of you," snapped Caution.

"Give my love to the lady," said MacTaggart. "If you've got good sense, you'll stop in France."

"For gas alone," said Caution.

"See you in Russia," retorted MacTaggart and at once severed the connection.

It gave Caution an odd feeling to know that MacTaggart and Ewell were winging this space not far away from them. And there were others, unseen, about them. Spanner, for instance. And those two boys out of Ohio, in their made-over low-wing speed job.

"This is easy," said Pam, hopefully. "We're riding against the sun. What time do we get into Paris?"

"Five tomorrow morning," said Caution, "if we're there on time."

"We'll be there," said Pam.

The night seemed to sweep across the seas to meet them, and then for long hours they could see nothing but the faint glow of their panel light. Pam dozed while Caution slept. Caution dozed while Pam slept.

40

And when the sun was cracking up over the rim of the world, they sighted Le Bourget Field.

A big gray ship was there on the tarmac. Men were running helter-skelter about it in an attempt to refuel swiftly. That was United States Airlines.

Another plane, a red one, was also ahead of them, getting ready to take off.

Caution waved the honor of landing to Pam. Pam was excited as she handled the big control wheel. She sent the ship slashing down at the runway like a javelin. She was elated because they had made the Atlantic crossing, they had cheated the sea.

The wheels crumped on the earth and they came to a stop, immediately besieged by the gas trucks and the mechanics who had been waiting for them.

The business of refueling went on apace. Pam, stretching her legs in the chilly morning air and sipping at a cup of scalding coffee, watched Ewell and MacTaggart getting ready to depart.

Caution drew out the bag of mail, gave it to a French official who stood ready with a canceling stamp, saw that each letter was favored and then took the bag back again.

The gurgle and hiss of gas was pleasing. Caution suddenly discovered that he was getting a whale of a kick out of all this. He was as excited as a schoolboy playing in his first varsity game.

Precious minutes were consumed in the check-over. Ewell and MacTaggart, eyeing them from afar, seemed pleased about something.

Neither Caution nor Pam saw a small boy clutching two objects—a hundred franc note and a large Graphic camera—approach their black plane. The small boy came from the other side of the ship. He opened the cabin door, tossed the camera gingerly into the dimness of the rear and departed.

Ewell and MacTaggart took off immediately afterward, their big gray ship rushing into the air with a space-devouring swoop.

Impatiently, Caution saw the last gas cap replaced and then slid in under the controls. Pam offered him a sandwich, but he was too excited to eat. Somehow he felt guilty at being excited.

They took off and built altitude quickly. The Eiffel Tower was a thin vertical line in the hazy distance. Pam saluted it soberly and then turned to watch ahead, in the hope of picking out the gray dot in the sky which would be Ewell and MacTaggart's ship.

Spanner and his green plane had been a little late in getting off, because of an overheating engine. His ship was almost invisible against the floor of the world far behind them.

"The Ohio boys didn't make it," said Caution.

Pam nodded sadly. That sea . . .

They stopped, after what seemed a very short jump, at Berlin, as a matter of form. They did not take on gas. They had their letters cancelled there, learned that the Ohio boys had been picked up at sea, learned that Ewell and MacTaggart had left ten minutes before.

Caution rubbed his hands together as Pam took off. "We gas at Warsaw, hit Moscow and then take the length of Russia."

Germany was a country of green and silver under them. They did not know when they crossed the border into Poland. Caution was flying with his trusted octant alone, and as long as he had the sun to shoot or stars to find, he was elated.

The motors were sweet, nothing stood in their way. It was almost too good to be true.

At Warsaw, a new supply of gas went into their tanks. Spanner was far behind them, but still plugging. Ewell and MacTaggart were just ahead. The length of Russia would be a deciding factor, and Caution knew that, with their two-hundred-mile-an-hour speed they would easily overtake the somewhat slower gray ship.

Caution sent their ship high after Warsaw. They crossed the Great Lowland Plain with a thirty-mile-an-hour wind pushing them along at eight thousand feet. Their twelve hundred horses were hammering air at a terrific rate.

They sighted a railroad at Pinsk, close to the border. It would lead them straight into Moscow. A chubby train, like some child's toy, laboring along beneath them, was soon left far behind and became at last no more than a puff of smoke.

By charging at the sun, they were losing daylight at a terrible rate. They would lose one entire day in the trip. While they had left Paris at five-thirty that morning, they were arriving in Moscow at five-thirty that afternoon, Moscow time, although it had taken them only nine hours to make the eighteen hundred miles.

43

When they landed in Moscow, they landed in trouble.

Caution set the big black plane on the runway of the great airport, joy in his heart. Ewell and MacTaggart were just taking off. If the Russians were fast in the refueling, the lead of the United States Airlines would be negligible.

The first thing Caution saw was a file of soldiers, all booted and helmeted, with fixed bayonets, walking toward them.

"I want gas," Caution said irritably to the lieutenant in charge, "and I want it fast. You've got your orders!"

"You," said the lieutenant, "are under arrest."

Thereupon, three soldiers laid down their rifles and snatched at Caution's arms.

Caution's dark eyes blazed. He threw off their hold and leaped to the ground. It was folly, he knew, and though he was conscious of Pam's small gasp, he gripped the lieutenant by the front of the tunic and shook him as one shakes a misbehaving child.

The soldiers immediately went into action. Caution felt bayonets nipping him from three sides.

"Don't let them kill you!" cried Pam.

Caution relented. The officer straightened his jacket and tried to appear unruffled.

"You have," he said in passable English, "one camera with which you snapped photographs of the Russian-Polish border. You are under arrest for a military crime. I'm ordered to bring you before a tribunal."

"Oh, lord!" moaned Caution. "Then take me, and be fast about it. I haven't got any camera. I don't know what you're talking about."

"You," said the lieutenant, "are under arrest."

Thereupon, two men climbed into the ship. They emerged a moment later, triumphantly bearing the black box of the Graphic. Pam stared at it as one stares at a snake.

Pleased, almost purring, the officer led Caution away. Pam, hope trying to pierce the gloom which had settled over her, used her winning way to persuade mechanics to refuel the ship.

She waited after that, not daring to breathe. Spanner landed, gave her a word of sympathy and took off again. A ship she had not known was in the race came down, helped her curse the Russians and went on.

Pam, walking nervously up and down in the dark, jumped at shadows and wondered what had happened to poor Caution. . . .

CHAPTER SEVEN

CAUTION BEATS A TRICK

CAUTION faced the three Soviet judges with his best possible face. "To prove this," said Caution, "you might develop the plates."

The three judges, looking like ogres out of a book of fairy tales, looked at one another and nodded at the suggestion. They felt ill at ease, detaining this man.

A photographer was found after a few minutes' search. He took the plates into his dark room. Caution waited and fumed. Minutes were precious.

After an age or two, the photographer brought in the plates, still dripping from the bath. They were pure white, unexposed. Caution heaved a sigh of relief.

They placed him in an official car and sent him back to the field. Pam received him by throwing her arms about his neck and sobbing violently.

They took off in the darkness, heavily loaded with gas, with only the feeble glare of the boundary lights to show them the way.

However, the Russian night was bright and Pam flew, while Caution figured out their course. The Ural Mountains passed under them, almost invisible save for a few upthrust peaks.

They headed out for the steppes, toward the Pacific, more than three hours behind Ewell and MacTaggart.

Thousands of miles of forest land, desert wastes, lazy rivers. It was cold at five thousand feet. Pam, wrapped in a long leather flying coat, sat back and looked ahead at the moon they raised out of the world. The moon was three times as big as it should have been, and a light orange color.

Pam looked sideways at Caution. He was half-asleep, watching the box which contained their robot. She wondered for a moment that he would trust the mechanical device.

He felt her eyes upon him and smiled at her. She felt warmed.

With a thirty-five-mile-an-hour wind to add to their two-hundred-mile pace, they were making two hundred and thirty-five. The beat of their wings resounded across the silent flatness of the world. They were alone in the immensity of space, and for all their smooth, swift flight, they seemed to hang motionless, suspended from the sky, like the moon.

Pam smiled back, although she was thinking about Ewell and MacTaggart. She wanted to beat them so much, after all they had done. She wanted so much to prove a small thing to Craig.

And then, suddenly, she realized that she wanted Caution to believe in her too.

Something was different about Caution, somehow. Using the robot, for instance. He hadn't trusted it at first.

Their next stop was Urga on the northern border of Mongolia, close beside the Gobi desert. There was gas to be had there.

In the morning, Caution roamed up and down the narrow aisle of the cabin. He had to bow his head to keep from banging it. He was restless and nervous, an odd state of affairs for him.

The rather complete interior yielded some cans, which he opened. He heated up coffee on an electric grill. Pam ate without comment, letting the robot fly the ship. Her eyes were searching the horizon before them, waiting for the dot which would mark a ship.

"This is traveling in luxury," said Caution.

He checked their position by a shot at the morning sun, gave the course a little more south and then let the robot fly some more. He whistled as he washed his face in a cupful of water. Looking at himself in a mirror, he decided he would need a shave. Odd to think of those things while lashing along at two hundred and thirty-five miles an hour. Odder still to be beating the sun at its own game.

The tan wastes of Mongolia, with the flat-topped, diminutive ranges of mountains, began to slide by under them. A camel caravan was strung out below, hardly moving. The drivers ran about in circles, excited and afraid.

"Don't worry," said Caution, as though they could hear him, "you'll be seeing this real often pretty soon."

Urga, with its chimneys, its railroads and its packed confines, appeared ahead of them. Pam decried the improvised field out on the edge of town.

Ewell and MacTaggart were already there.

"We've caught up to them!" Pam said exultantly.

When they landed, brown-faced Mongolians swarmed about them. The gasoline was in sealed drums.

MacTaggart, looking very surly, came near to Caution.

"You may have got this far, but you won't be getting much farther, my friend Jones."

Caution started over to him, but Pam caught his arm. "Save your energy," said Pam, surprised at this second show of temper and pugnacity on Caution's part.

It seemed that Ewell and MacTaggart always managed to beat them to the takeoff. Their gray ship went away first this time, swooping upward into the yellow sky of morning, lost almost instantly in the haze.

When Pam and Caution got off, Pam said, "I wonder what they're cooking up now."

Caution shrugged, as much as to say, let them bring it on, whatever it is. He looked grim.

They picked up the gray dot ahead of them, and the margin between began to narrow down.

Their radio buzzed. Caution took up the phone.

"Calling TCA ship," said a thin, despairing voice out of nowhere.

"Jones speaking," said Caution, setting the dial.

"Hello. This is Spanner. I'm cracked up about a hundred miles short of Kanchow. Would you carry the report in for me? Like a good fellow?"

"Sure," said Caution. "Too bad, Spanner. You hurt?"

"No, not much. Motor conked. It's been overheating for the last thousand miles. But I'm out of the race. Good luck, you lucky bum!"

"I'll see you're picked up," said Caution.

Pam shook her head. "Poor kid! He was leading, too!"

It struck neither of them that their sympathy was out of place in a struggle of this sort. They were an integral part of the flying brotherhood. In that moment, they would gladly have had Spanner win.

Mongolia faded behind them. The great bean fields of Manchuria began to pass by in the moonlight, and then they caught sight of the very yellow Yellow Sea, stretching limitless out to the horizon, blazing under the great orange disc of the moon.

Pam smiled ecstatically. Ewell and MacTaggart were dropping their lead swiftly. Before many hours would pass, they would be in Yokohama. After that—the Pacific!

They crossed the last of the Japan Sea in the dawn, coming into sight of those innumerable terraced islands, all green and infinitely detailed, with toy houses, toy boats and dolls for people.

The small fishing smacks—with their square bows and sterns and their fragile-appearing latticed sails—went serenely on their courses, as though unaware of any such thing as a speeding transport ship.

At Yokohama they saw the half-moon harbor, the breakwater, the rows and rows of anchored ships, the factory chimneys, the carelessly winding streets and the postage-stamp-sized airport where they were to refuel for the final water jump.

When they came down, they saw Ewell and MacTaggart again. They seemed always fated to tag their rivals' speeding wings.

The Japanese had gas trucks, but no chamois gas strainers.

51

Caution tried to explain matters to an interpreter, but succeeded ill.

"But," said the interpreter doggedly, "this is good gas. Why should one strain it?"

Caution gave in, much to Pam's surprise. "Fill it up—and fast," said Caution.

The gas gurgled in, a truck full of it. Caution busied himself with cleaning plugs and adjusting carburetors. He came back to the cabin triumphant and covered with grease.

"They're holding up fine, those engines. We won't wait for an overhaul."

Pam was again amazed. She was silent when they took off. She was not especially tired. With the robot to take the heavy work of flying, and with the softness of the seats to sleep in, the plane was as comfortable as a one-room apartment.

Staid Caution—what had happened to him?

They flashed out across the blue, serene Pacific, heading a little more to the north now, ready to pick up the first fueling station in the Aleutian Islands.

The day was fine and clear and Caution was elated, in spite of a slight cross wind which made navigation more difficult. However, he told himself, their luck was holding.

Hour after hour they winged their way above the sea, smooth, powerful flight. And then things began to happen.

The starboard engine began to wheeze plaintively, missing a beat every few moments. Caution sat up straight. His lips were tightly compressed. Had they come this far only to make a forced landing in the sea?

Pam watched him call Yokohama, listening to that motor at the same time.

"TCA plane calling Yokohama. Calling Yokohama."

Yokohama, in the form of a round-the-world liner, answered him with swift concern.

"Motor going bad," said Caution. "Might have to land in sea. Position, hundred and eightieth meridian, fifty-one degrees, seven minutes north latitude. Please stand by."

But he knew the liner's task of finding them in all this sea would be hopeless.

The ship flew on, slower now because of the faulty engine, but it still flew. The Pacific, as night darkened, no longer looked serene. It was an ugly black sheet, a waiting beast who slept until he was ready to receive them.

Caution thought hard, scowling and rubbing his jaw. Then, with sudden decision, he motioned Pam to the controls.

"There's water in that gas," said Caution. "There's a drain under each wing. The gas will be on top, and I can drain the water out."

Pam gasped. Was this Caution?

Before she could stop him, he opened the door, caught hold of a jury strut. Wrench in hand, he leaned far out over the dragging emptiness and opened the drain petcock. The slipstream tore at him, ripped his shirt from his back. A fine spray whisked out of the opening.

He let it run from the wing tank for a moment and then, when he could hold on no longer, he wrapped his legs about the strut and closed the drain.

He came inside in a moment to face a very white Pam. Caution was grinning. He had cheated Old Man Death.

"Gee," said Caution, "that was fun!"

The motor ran better after that. Caution paid it no further heed. In the lavatory at the back of the cabin he washed himself up, even combed his hair.

At ten o'clock they switched on their powerful landing lights and headed down toward the lighted beacon of the Andreanof Islands, in the Aleutians.

They landed on a strip of beach and were immediately approached by an old man with a straggling beard, the keeper of the gas cache.

He peered at them a moment and then said, "Trans-Continental Airlines, huh? Then let's see—that's your bunch of gas over there to the right, under that tarp."

"Why that lot?" said Caution, a little curious.

"That's the stack I laid out for you and that's the stack you'll take." The old man's voice was whining, petulant.

"All right," said Caution, "get your ax and let's go."

"I opened them for you, so's you wouldn't lose time."

Caution stood there in the flash of the landing lights and studied him. "*You* opened them?"

"Yes. What you going to do about it?"

"Which cache belongs to Ewell and MacTaggart?"

"That other one. I'm not supposed to get them mixed."

"Then I'll take theirs and they can have mine."

There was a quick movement of the man's hand. Caution suddenly found himself staring into the muzzle of an ancient revolver.

"Take that gas," grated the man.

Caution's lips were tight. His left eye was half closed. He looked exactly like his father.

He lunged to one side. The gun flamed. Caution grabbed the wrist, hammered a solid punch into the man's face. The fellow dropped like a felled ox.

Caution immediately ran to the pile of cans. The quantity of gas was tremendous. He despaired of time. However, Pam was beside him in a moment. Together they carried more than a ton of gasoline and dumped it into the tanks of the ship.

Carrying those cans by the red glow of the fire and the whiteness of the landing lights, they looked like two gnomes struggling with immense burdens.

Every few moments, Caution would give vent to a chuckle, and when they had almost finished, he had to laugh outright.

Pam's ears caught the roar of an approaching engine. "It's Ewell and MacTaggart! Let's go!"

They dumped the last two cans and then swung into their cabin. The big black plane took off with a snarling roar, charging up into the blackness of night, just as the red and green running lights of the other plane showed close at hand.

"Now," said Pam, "what were you laughing at?"

"I'll tell you later," said Caution.

CHAPTER EIGHT

Batty Jones' Son

THEY flew the remainder of that night, all the next day, seeing only sea. No steamers; nothing but water. The weather favored them, and they struck neither storm nor headwinds.

At seven the following evening, they sighted Vancouver Island in all its greenness, and at nine they were swooping down upon the airport to the south of Seattle, on the tide flats.

They were tiring, nerves jumpy with the incessant roar of the engines. They marveled that they had stood it so well this far. But there had been two of them, and they had had the robot working. They had slept sitting, but slept fairly well.

At Seattle they paused long enough to get a hot meal. Then they headed east. They tried time and again to check the whereabouts of Ewell and MacTaggart, but they failed.

Fifteen hours from Seattle to New York, having the wind behind them. All night and all day.

At four-thirty that afternoon they landed at Floyd Bennett Field, letting down their landing gear for one last time.

For the last three hours Pam had been sleeping. She brightened now as they coasted to a stop before the operations office.

A swarm of people, spreading out across the field like

57

a wide black sheet, besieged their plane. Police held them back. A car mercifully came and took them directly out of the ship.

Craig was there, waiting for them, his bushy hair standing straight up, red face alight with joy.

When they were left alone in the administration building, Craig scooped Pam into his arms and held her for a long, long time. He smoothed her rumpled yellow hair.

"It was swell," said Craig, and there were tears in his eyes. "I . . . I never knew before, but for days I've been thinking about you, worrying about you. They were buying up my stock, trying to ruin me, and all the time I was thinking I'd be left with nothing if you failed.

"And then suddenly I realized I wouldn't be really ruined. I could still do something, anything, but more than that I knew I . . . knew I had you, Pam. I guess I've been so busy making money I forgot about my girl."

She was beaming, all weariness vanished from her. This was what she had wanted. This was what she had been waiting for.

The crowd was seeping into the room and they moved on to Caution's office. Caution swept the accumulated papers from the desk with one single thrust. They scattered out across the floor in a grand mess. He slumped down in his chair and put his feet on the desk, closing his eyes for a moment, as though he steadied himself.

"Craig," said Caution, without noticing that Craig was puzzled and aghast at this sudden easiness of manner, that Craig was watching that down-drooping mouth and that squinted eye. "Craig, I think you're going to have to get a new general manager. I'm sorry, but I'm not fit for the job. And besides—"

"Not fit!" Craig gaped.

"No. I told you about my dad. I found out a week ago that I wasn't thinking right. All these years I've been holding myself down. Well, the Batty Jones in me licked the Caution."

"You're crazy!" cried Craig.

"Yeah," said Caution. "Crazy. I've always been crazy. I've made myself be a trained robot because I thought it was right. That's over. I've saved money, plenty of it. I'm going to pilot out some new routes that would surprise you. I'm going to—"

He was interrupted by the roar of an engine. Pam looked up, and then smiled.

It was Ewell and MacTaggart.

The gray ship came in for a sloppy landing. A car went up to it through the crowd and presently Ewell and MacTaggart were in the operation office, flame in their eyes. They were like men who have borne too much; their eyes were red, their jaws set in an ugly line.

Caution went out of his office to meet them. He, too, was weaving on his feet.

Ewell roared a mighty curse and stamped close to Caution. "You low-down skunk! You're a dirty, sneaking, double-crossing dog! I'll see that you get it!"

He was heedless of the Department of Commerce men standing near, unaware that the aviation world was right at his hand.

MacTaggart, oversized head wobbling, screamed, "You stole our gas!"

59

Eyebrows went up. Caution grinned—a deadly grin.

"I took the gas that was left for you, yes. I left you my gas."

"You damned thieving devil! You knew your gas was dirty. You knew it had water in it. You wanted to make us use it!"

"Everybody knows your firm took the gas up there," said Caution, grinning. "If my gas was bad, then how was it yours was good? It was the same gas."

Ewell started. He was so fogged that he had not sensed the presence of others. A snicker went up. A pair of officials came close, frowning.

Ewell knew then that it was all over. He and MacTaggart were through. The NAA and the Department of Commerce and the rest would attend to United States Airlines.

Suddenly, MacTaggart sprang forward, snarling. Ewell came with him. Caution rocked forward and slammed a heavy fist into Ewell's mouth. Not wishing to hit a smaller man, Caution tripped MacTaggart.

Ewell came back like a mad bull, arms flailing. Caution hit him a precise blow over the eye, drawing blood. The second blow was not felt by Ewell. He was out on his feet, sagging slowly to the floor. The officials took charge.

"The fool!" muttered Craig.

"Yeah, I thought that was in the wind," said Caution. "I'll look them both up tomorrow and we'll have a real fight!"

"Not tomorrow," said Pam.

"No? What's happening tomorrow?"

"We've got to get to work on the details of this route. TCA has it in the bag. We'll have to start it again."

"Nuts!" said Caution. "Leave that to trained robots. Me?

60

I'm going to start out for some real flying. I mean to have some fun at this racket for a change. I've pushed too many buttons and dictated too many letters."

"But, Caution," said Pam, "we've got to map this line. We have to hire new pilots and— Gee whiz, Caution, come down to earth! Stunts never did anything for aviation!"

Suddenly Caution reached out and gathered her tired body to him. He held her cradled in his arms and walked slowly toward a waiting car. Craig beamed.

Caution stopped in the doorway. He didn't seem to realize that the place was filled with people. Very deliberately he kissed Pam.

"Oh!" she said.

"I've been meaning to for some time," said Caution.

"It looks like I lose a general manager," said Craig, to no one in particular, "but," and he smiled broadly, "I'm gaining a wild son-in-law!"

BOOMERANG BOMBER

BOOMERANG BOMBER

"AHOY down there!" bellowed Clint Ragen into the gaping hold. "What are you doing with that bomber?"

The blotchy-faced second officer glanced up, shrugged, and turned to direct the hoisting of a large boxed assemblage. The winch started slowly, went faster, and then, like a projectile, the box swooped over and thumped on the biggest concrete dock in Kobe, Japan.

Clint Ragen swore loudly and whirled to run up the ladder to the bridge. The liner's captain was waiting, evidently with prepared answers.

"What's the idea?" roared Clint. "You can't land that plane here. I've paid freight all the way to Shanghai."

The captain shrugged immaculate blue-clad shoulders. "I'm not delaying my ship just for one piece of freight, Mr. Ragen, and although I realize that you should have been notified of this sooner—"

"Come to the point," snapped Clint.

"Just this. The Japanese have branded your bomber as being contraband of war, and we cannot sail unless we unload it immediately."

"Con-contraband of war!" Clint stared wide-eyed at the dock. "But they . . . can't do . . ."

The appearance of a small frock-coated, gray-haired

American stopped Clint's flow of words. Clint recognized Professor Alan Simpson, late of Kansas City, and a fellow passenger.

"My dear fellow," said the professor, "I would strongly advise your going down there to supervise that unloading. I saw the first crate splinter on the side." Simpson pointed with his umbrella and nodded, as though satisfied that he had done his duty.

Clint Ragen whirled on the captain again. "Damn it, man, you can't pitch that plane off here! Do you know that it's worth seventy thousand dollars? If I don't deliver it to the Nationalist government, I'll be fired. I'm responsible for it, and so are you. It's in your care as freight."

"Sue, if you want to," said the captain, wearily. "It would cost more than that to hold this boat up any longer. I'm already behind my schedule. You better see the Japanese authorities."

Clint took a deep breath and glared. His fists clenched and unclenched below the lower edge of his white jacket. Suddenly he yanked his Panama over his eyes and ran for the gangway.

"Those crates marked 'Engine'—" began Professor Simpson, before he realized that the pilot had gone. He turned to say something to the captain and found that he, too, had departed, in all his gold-braid magnificence. Professor Simpson lifted off his tinted glasses, wiped them, and moved to the rail.

Clint Ragen was trying his best to prevent damage to his expensive charge. The plane was crated in sections which were now being strewn aimlessly about on the concrete. Coolies stood by listlessly watching the performance, quite willing to lend a hand, but not knowing where to start. The pilot bawled at them in English, but they shook their heads, raised their eyebrows and remained standing idle.

Professor Simpson shouted something in a reedy voice, and the coolies glanced up. At another shout, they went busily to work, piling the crates neatly under the eaves of the shed.

Clint Ragen stood still in surprise and stared at the slight old man who had worked the magic. "If you speak this lingo—" began Clint.

"I'll come down," said Professor Simpson. "The guard is coming, and I doubt if any of them will be able to speak English or Chinese." He went carefully down the slanted gangway and came to a stop beside the pilot. Deliberately, he wiped his glasses, replaced them and stared around him.

The last box swooped dockward in a net, to be deftly caught and placed with the others. Then the guard came up and clanked rifle butts to the concrete. The officer in charge was smartly uniformed. His leather shone, and his bristly hair stood straight up into his pillbox cap. A small pair of wings graced his chest.

The officer spoke rapidly to Clint, and when he had finished, the professor translated. "He says that this bombing airplane is contraband of war and has been seized by the Japanese government. He wants to know if you are the owner."

Clint stepped back and compressed his lips, his fists working. "Tell him I am the man who is responsible for the safe delivery of this bomber. And tell him that the US will raise merry hell with the Rising Sun if anything happens to said US property."

The professor spoke and received an answer from the

officer. "You are in error," Simpson told Clint. "This bomber is intended for the Chinese government and is therefore war contraband. It is all very simple, Mr. Ragen. You have no alternative but to board the liner and leave your airplane here."

"What?" shouted Ragen. "Go away and leave seventy thousand dollars' worth of airplane? Why, my company would kill me in cold blood. Do you realize that—oh, hell! I can't let myself be marooned here in Japan, and I've got to deliver that plane if I have to fight the whole Japanese army. Tell him that and ask how in hell they knew it was aboard, anyway."

Professor Simpson, with quite a bit of editing, translated the message, and the Japanese flying officer became very stiff and stern. He frowned, but before he could open his mouth to speak, a whistle blasted above them, drowning out all other sound.

Clint Ragen moved one step forward, and then stopped. It was no use, now. The liner was already thirty feet away from the pier, and retreating faster every moment. The captain, afraid for his ship and cargo, had not waited, knowing that the outcome could be in only one side's favor—the Japanese.

The slight, gray-haired Simpson stood and trembled violently. Words quivered in his throat, but were never uttered. Professor Simpson knew that he had been marooned without baggage or passport. Slowly, the professor turned his lined face to Clint.

"My passport!" he finally said. "My baggage! I will arrive in Shanghai too late to join my Gobi expedition. I am a ruined man, Mr. Ragen!"

Clint Ragen, though worried over his own troubles, was

instantly sympathetic. "I'm sorry about that. It was I who brought you down here. See here, Simpson, I've got some money with me, and you're welcome to as much of that as you need. They won't raise the devil with you for not having a passport. Not you, they won't. I always carry mine right with me."

"I forgot mine," grieved Simpson. He patted a binocular case on his hip, and hefted his black folded umbrella. "These are all the baggage that I have."

The pilot pushed a twenty-dollar bill in Simpson's hand and sighed deeply. "Tell this monkey to take me to some officials. I want to talk with somebody high up, and I want to see the US ambassador."

Simpson jabbered rapidly, listened closely, and then said, "You cannot communicate with your ambassador because he is not available. The only officials to whom you may speak are the high officers of the air force. I would suggest—"

"Tell him to take me to that outfit," said Ragen. "And tell them to post a guard over these crates. We'll find out whether or not a bomber is contraband."

Baron Suga sat high upon a raised platform and studied the Americans who had been brought in before the impromptu court. He saw that one of the foreigners was tall, blond, dressed in a soiled duck suit and Panama hat. From this man's bearing, the Japanese officer knew that he had here a military personality. Of the other foreigner, the baron understood that he must be one of great learning and dignity.

Looking up, Clint Ragen understood in his turn that

something was about to go hard with him. In the polished faces he saw neither mercy nor compromise. Nevertheless, his lean features bore a somewhat insolent expression. Clint Ragen considered himself quite up to any situation which might arise, and in spite of the braid on the baron's uniform, Clint Ragen knew he faced only a man.

Baron Suga leaned forward and spoke in clipped English. "Your name is Ragen. You are a pilot. You were formerly a captain in the United States Army Air Service. You intend to deliver a bomber to the Chinese and then fly it for them."

Some of the insolence went out of the pilot's face. His sea blue eyes shifted warily, and he thought to himself that Japanese Intelligence must be very thorough to know all that about one man.

"The bomber," continued Baron Suga, "is, according to an ultimatum issued recently, contraband of war. Your act in delivering it to the Chinese may be regarded, for our purposes, as unfriendly. Why did you not accept it as such and proceed with your vessel?"

Clint Ragen shoved his hands deep into his coat pockets, and shifted his weight to his right foot. "Because said vessel ran off and left us," he said curtly.

"And this man with you," said the baron, bowing respectfully toward Professor Simpson. "Why did he find it necessary to accompany you before this aviation board?"

"Because my ship left me," stated Simpson, removing his glasses and wiping them, squinting his eyes the while. "I know nothing of Japan. I have no friends here."

"And yet," snapped Baron Suga, "you speak Japanese."

"I learned it in Kansas," apologized the professor. "I had a servant boy who was Japanese, and he taught me. I always learn what presents itself to me for consideration."

A young flying officer leaned toward the baron and whispered in his ear. Then the baron bowed to Professor Simpson. "My apologies for my suspicion. You are from Kansas, then?"

Clint Ragen walked forward half a dozen paces, until he could place his hand on the shoulder-high desktop. "He's all right. He was going to lead an expedition into the Gobi. What I want to know is this—what are you going to do with the bomber?"

Baron Suga permitted himself a smile. "First, I believe we are concerned with you. I find in you a former army officer who has committed an unfriendly act, and is perhaps, even now, contemplating espionage."

The pilot stood straighter, and his eyes hardened. "You can't get away with that. You'll either return that bomber to me for shipment, or I'll have your hide. Understand?"

"Speak softly, Mr. Ragen," admonished the baron.

"Softly, hell! I'm delivering a bomber to the Chinese, and I'm going to deliver it. That ship is worth seventy thousand dollars."

The baron shrugged. "It carries a useful load of ten tons, has two five-fifty horsepower engines, and can fly nine hundred and fifty miles. What chance has our army if you hand such machines as this to the Chinese?"

71

Clint Ragen had the appearance of a man harried beyond resistance. His eyes had receded until they were two blue slits and his fingernails dug deeply into his palms.

"Listen," said the pilot, slowly, deliberately. "China is buying her ships from reliable companies, and she's paying cash. You have a plane here you call the Kawasaki KDA-5. It is a copy of the Curtiss Hawk. You have another plane called the Nakajima 92, which is a copy of a French Morane."

"What of it?" shrugged the baron.

"Just this," Clint roared. "You're too damned dumb to build your own planes. You've got to copy those of other nations, but China shoots square with us. She pays for our ships, instead of stealing our designs."

Baron Suga's face deepened in color. His mouth fell open, exhibiting sharp teeth. Unexpectedly, he lashed out and slapped Clint Ragen across the face. But the pilot did not wait to see what else would happen. His fist soared up before the baron's face could withdraw, and the baron slammed back, lips spouting blood.

A young flying officer pitched himself bodily at the American, hands outstretched, eyes glittering. But before he could connect, Clint Ragen's fist had hammered out again, and the pilot was down. A soldier raised his rifle, but before he could pull the trigger, someone knocked it aside.

Then a pistol butt caught the American on the side of the head, stunning him. Before he could recover, men were all over him, pinning him down.

"Take him," said Baron Suga, "to a prison. Allow him

to communicate with no one. You have insulted officers of Japan, Mr. Ragen, and soon you will discover just what that means."

They dragged the pilot out of the room and left Professor Simpson wringing his hands. "Oh, dear!" he moaned. "You won't . . . you won't . . ."

"No," said Baron Suga. "If you promise us your silence, worthy sir, you will have your liberty."

"Thank you," said the professor, and tottered from the room, leaning heavily upon his umbrella.

Clint Ragen was up at dawn. Not that there was anything to do, but he had been unable to sleep on the hard board and wooden pillow which constituted his bed. With a long, sleepless night of pondering behind him, Clint Ragen had begun to appreciate the seriousness of his circumstances. He had heartily cursed himself for his verbal and fistic outbreak before the aviation officers, but that did him no good now.

The cell was not very big, but Clint paced what there was of it. The chances were against his getting to see the ambassador or even a consul. Clint was under no delusions as to the actual reasons behind the seizure of the plane. That sweet bomber would look quite well with the blood-red disk of Japan on its wings.

In the eyes of international law, Clint Ragen was a gunrunner, and appalling things happened to gentlemen who pursued that hectic trade. There were guns in those crates—late-model machine guns which were to serve as armament for the ship. And Japan's declaration concerning arms had been made while Clint was aboard that old-fashioned tub.

So now, in short, Clint Ragen was as good—or as bad—as a criminal in the eyes of Japan and, subsequently, in the eyes of the United States.

But Clint's ponderings were interrupted by a light tap, a grate of iron on stone, and the whisper of cloth. Someone was coming down the corridor which led to the cell.

Clint tensed, waiting, wondering what message might be forthcoming. Then he swore and sat back dejectedly on his wooden bunk. Professor Simpson was staring through the small window in the door.

"Well?" Clint asked.

Simpson removed his glasses, wiped them, put them back, and took a deep breath. "Good morning, Mr. Ragen. You do not appear to have spent a comfortable night."

Clint grunted. "Slept like a daisy."

"I believe I have news for you," continued Simpson. "The officers have charitably offered you a compromise."

"What's this?"

Simpson coughed hollowly. "They are thinking of giving you a military court-martial."

"Firing squad?"

"Well," the professor hesitated, "not exactly. Perhaps that might be, too. But instead of that, they are quite willing that you should go free."

"What's the joker?" snapped Clint, moving near.

"You see, yesterday afternoon, they tried to put the bomber together, and, as I understand it, they encountered some difficulty. The matter is a complicated one, I presume."

"Complicated!" Clint snorted. "All they have to do is pull it out of the crates, buckle on the wings, mount the motors and fasten the props. I'm afraid you got 'em wrong, Professor."

"No, I don't believe I did. It seems there is some difficulty. I don't exactly understand it, but the motors won't fit the mounts."

"Huh! They probably don't know when they're right side up." Clint moved restlessly. "Well, what's that got to do with me?"

"They asked me to tell you . . ." began Simpson. "They want you to put the . . . er . . . to put the plane together for them."

Clint let out an explosive sound. His eyes flamed. "You mean they've got the crust to—now let me get this straight, Simpson. They want me to fix up the ship they swiped off me. That right?"

"Yes," agreed the professor, obviously relieved.

"Well, you can tell them for me that they can go straight to hell. I suppose they want me to buy gasoline for it, too."

The professor began to wring his hands. "But, my dear fellow, can't you see, don't you understand that they will drop all charges if you will do this for them? I do not believe that you fully appreciate what you face."

Clint grated his teeth and started to swear, but suddenly he checked himself, eyes narrow, speculative.

75

"All right," he said, suddenly. "Go back and tell them that I'll be right with them as soon as they let me out."

"Ah!" said Simpson. "I thought you would listen."

The aviation field was nearly the best Japan had to offer along such lines. Here the Inland Sea and the jagged islands made flying a very difficult task, for emergency fields did not exist. In the United States, such a field as that on which Clint Ragen now found himself would have been a poor substitute. The equipment was modern enough, and the hangars were large, but the runways were short and uneven. Bordered on each side by rice paddies, the ground was soggy.

A file of soldiers waited to take the foreign pilot into custody. They marched him out to the detached pile of segments which, when assembled, would be the bomber. Clint stopped short and snorted loudly.

Professor Simpson, bringing up the rear, also stopped.

"Tell them," Clint said to the professor, "that they might at least mount the wheels on the fuselage before they try to fasten on the wings."

Simpson caught the attention of a young flying officer and passed the message along. Orders were rapped, and the half-braced wings came off and the wheels started to go on. Clint stood by sullenly, watching the greasy mechanics swarm over seventy thousand dollars' worth of plane. Then his professional pride got the better of him, and he pulled off his coat and waded in.

With the landing gear attended to, Clint stepped back

and told the professor the proper directions for mounting the wing. Simpson translated in a monotonous voice, leaning heavily on his umbrella, his gray hair rustling beneath his black hat.

"If my chiefs could see me now," said Clint, "a firing squad would be tame. I'm mad enough to tear into this whole outfit."

"I would strongly advise against it," the professor said. "There are several armed men in the immediate vicinity."

Clint stepped forward to help take a mighty engine out of its cradle. With his hands full of spare parts, he tried to point to the motor's destination, but the mechanics stared blankly at him. Clint looked around for the professor, but that worthy, for the moment, had disappeared. The pilot shrugged, and did the best he could with sign language.

With engines one and two mounted, Clint stepped back, to discover that the professor was again with him. He took the opportunity to outline the procedure for mounting a prop, and then, the minute Clint's back was turned, Simpson was once more gone.

When the propeller was hubbed, the professor was back.

"Damn!" said Clint, "I wish you wouldn't do a Houdini every time I need you. What's the matter?"

Simpson merely fumbled nervously with the binocular case and said nothing.

The afternoon wore away, but each passing moment saw the bomber closer to completion. The motors were in place; the wings were on; control wires had been slipped over their pulleys, and Clint was adding a few finishing touches.

Six machine guns, lately covered with Cosmoline, were now laid out on a strip of canvas, shining under the slanted rays of the departing sun. Clint carried a brace up to a cockpit and fastened them down upon their mount. A Japanese flying officer was all attention.

"He wants," said Simpson, "to know how to load them."

Clint obliged. One of his boxes divulged a dozen loaded drums. Carefully, he inserted the belts and pulled them through the breeches.

"Tell him—" Clint began, but looked up in time to see that the professor had once more disappeared. He scratched his head irritably and began to demonstrate at length in pantomime.

With the guns all mounted, Clint climbed down, and found Simpson again at his elbow.

"That fellow," said the professor, pointing to another flying officer, "is anxious to find out where you fill the gasoline tanks."

Clint nodded wearily as he saw a large fuel truck rumble up to the side of the ship. Hoses were tossed to the pilot, and one by one he filled the tanks, amid the exclamations of the onlookers. They had never before seen auxiliary tanks in a ship's wing. Once started, Clint filled them all.

An officer wanted to know exactly how the controls worked, and exactly what all the meters stood for. With a sigh, Clint sat in the pilot's seat and demonstrated. The pilot looked around for his interpreter, but once more he found Simpson to be among the missing.

However, he was not needed, for here was one flying officer who spoke an understandable brand of English.

"You've been very kind," said the Japanese pilot. "Now would you please start the engines? I would like to know how that is done."

Clint started them, one by one, and sent their blast rocketing about the hills of the Inland Sea. He pointed to the gauges which showed when the engines were warm. Then, letting them idle, he leaned back, tired from the day's work.

The officer smiled thinly. "You have been very kind. Now, perhaps, we had better restore you to the prison."

"The prison!" snapped Clint. "I thought—"

"Yes, but you were not right. We still have grave charges to press against you."

Clint sat up straight, and something in his eyes made the officer hastily draw a pistol from his belt. Then there came a shriek from the hangars, and the sound of pounding feet. The officer turned, and over his shoulder Clint saw Professor Simpson racing toward the bomber, umbrellaless, hatless, and very hard of face.

To think was to act. Clint snatched the pistol from the officer's hand and slammed him in the jaw. He dumped the Japanese out onto the ground, reaching down with the same movement to help Simpson into the pit. But Simpson needed no help. He scrambled in like a scared rabbit, leaped over the cockpit combing and slithered down into the observer's pit behind.

Clint fired twice at men who were trying to catch hold

79

of the wings. Two throttles went all the way down on their arcs, and the plane began to rumble forward, shaking in every section.

"What the hell—" Clint started to shout, but a machine gun near the hangar opened up, and the bomber took the air.

Another machine gun started to bark, but this time it was just in back of the pilot's head. He turned for an instant, to see Simpson fumbling with the loaded guns. Clint didn't know what possible trouble Simpson could have gotten into, but the bomber's wheels were off, and the trouble didn't matter. Back on the tarmac, fighting planes were being rammed out and started. Without a good gunner to cover his tail, Clint knew he was in for a hot time of it.

As quickly as possible, he built altitude and began to fly southwest. He watched the skies about him for the first signs of the attack he knew would come. Those Japanese pursuit planes could make close to two hundred miles an hour, and the bomber was going top speed at a hundred and eighty.

The two machine guns mounted in front of him were empty, but, reaching back for drums, Clint quickly remedied that. He was hard put to keep his eyes open against the beating slipstream, and his hair persisted in whipping down over his face. And then a helmet plopped down beside him, and without asking questions, he put it on.

Dusk was upon the world below him. The blue waters of the Inland Sea were stretching out, cut here and there by terraced islands. But Clint was not looking at the beauty of it.

He was worried about the bomber, for he knew that it hadn't been test flown, and that in the event of a crash, he would have to ride it down.

And then the first Japanese Kawasaki KDA-5 plummeted out of the sky and sizzled past the bomber. The pursuit pilot banked sharply and, above the engines' roar, Clint could hear the stutter of guns. Another plane shot down and came up again, tracer streaking through its prop.

The guns in the observer's pit began to chatter. Clint pressed his own trips and tried to angle the heavy bomber into firing position, but he could not stunt such a ship. He could only plow ahead and trust to luck.

The interplane struts of the leading Kawasaki suddenly disappeared. Before Clint could grasp that miracle, the plane was spinning. It would get down all right, but in a very tattered condition.

Another Kawasaki lanced by, but it was not firing. Clint could see the pilot jerking vainly at the loose stick. That fellow would also have a tough time bringing his ship back. A third pursuit ship zoomed past Clint's nose, and he pressed his trips. The prop went out in a shower of splinters, and the maimed motor began to shake loose from its mount. Clint grinned. He'd show those guys!

Three ships in formation lanced out of nowhere, guns hammering, motors howling, wires screaming. They came like javelins, but before they reached the altitude of the bomber, the lead plane slipped harshly. Then the second skidded, and the third went into a spin. Clint's eyes bulged.

*The pursuit pilot banked sharply and, above the engines' roar,
Clint could hear the stutter of guns.*

An ambitious pilot dived down and leveled off, streaking directly for the great plane's nose. Clint fired three short bursts straight into the other's prop. And then the air was full of smoke. Far below, a parachute opened. The flaming ruin of the pursuit Kawasaki sent a black geyser of water into the hovering night.

Clint realized that darkness was settling rapidly. He could hear other motors, but he could not spot them, and he knew, in turn, that he could not be spotted. He sat back, relaxing, and began to worry about his destination.

Without a navigator, even though the flight to Shanghai was only eight hundred miles, Clint did not know where he would end up. Besides, he was entirely too worn out for five and a half hours of flying. Allowing for that and his lack of charts, he did not believe he could possibly reach Shanghai. It was a bad end to a glorious career. He'd go down in the Yellow Sea, and there wouldn't even be wreckage to mark his passing.

He groaned to himself and wondered what in the name of all the Japanese devils had caused him to escape. There'd be a price on his head, now. Some of those Kawasakis had been crashed, that was certain, and even if the pilots hadn't been killed, the offense was great. However, that wouldn't make too much difference with the Chinese. They might give him a raise in pay for it, in fact. But then, of course, he'd never get to China.

A slithering sensation against his right arm made him look up. He saw that Professor Simpson had slid down into the front cockpit, and was settling himself into the copilot's seat.

Clint Ragen saw the small man begin to wipe his face with a handkerchief. He thrust the glasses into his pocket and ran his fingers through his hair. And then he pulled a small map and an octant out of his frock coat and snapped on the panel light. That done, he stood up and held the navigation instrument to his eye, writing on a pad.

There was a sliding panel which closed in the cockpit, and Simpson drew this over, shutting out most of the engines' noise.

"Fly 221 degrees," said Simpson in a crisp, clear voice. "That'll slam Shanghai right on the old nose. Allowing for drift, it'll take five hours and forty-five minutes. If you're tired, old boy, I'll push her along."

Clint Ragen frowned. He was puzzled by the professor's use of slang, and more puzzled by the change in his tone of voice. He turned and looked squarely, and what he saw made his eyes widen perceptibly.

Professor Simpson's gray hair was now black. There were no lines on his face, and without them, the expression was youthful and eager. Simpson looked very military and businesslike.

"Just who the hell are you?" Clint asked, amazed.

"Lieutenant Brandon, United States Navy."

"But why the—oh, I get it." Clint grinned. "You sure had me going for a while. I thought you were just what you said you were. You Intelligence boys sure do run into some awful scrapes. I was with the Army Intelligence over the Mexican border for a while."

"But," said Brandon, alias Simpson, "I'm afraid I led you an awful chase, with some bad risks. To get you out to the field to assemble the ship, I told them they'd break it if they didn't know how. You see, I had orders to get photographs of a Japanese airdrome and the landmarks around it, and I didn't even think I'd better give it a try until they had your ship thrown over the side. That sure simplified things. I got some beauties of pictures." He patted the binocular case.

Clint Ragen looked at him and grinned. "Well, thanks, anyway. I'd never have lived it down if they'd gotten this bomber. But I still don't see how they knew it was aboard the old tub."

"No?" grinned the Navy man. "One of our chaps tipped 'em off to give me a chance to get out to the field!"

STORY PREVIEW

STORY PREVIEW

NOW that you've just ventured through some of the captivating tales in the Stories from the Golden Age collection by L. Ron Hubbard, turn the page and enjoy a preview of *Hurtling Wings*. Join racer and test pilot Cal Bradley as he flies in the National Air Meet to capture valuable air mail contracts. But Cal faces an unscrupulous competitor and a gorgeous dame who may spell his ruin as the planes take flight.

HURTLING WINGS

"THREE hundred miles an hour is too fast for anybody," said Georgia Kyle positively, but Cal only poised for the briefest instant on the catwalk of his racing plane to answer.

"Somebody will do it and it might as well be yours truly." With that, he lowered himself into his pit and pulled his goggles down over his forehead.

The girl's long black lashes dropped uncertainly down over her eyes, her face startlingly white under the jet of her hair. She looked up again and saw the picture Cal Bradley made sitting there in the narrow confines of his "office." She saw his striped helmet, his brown leather jacket, his frank blue eyes and his rugged face—the face of a man born to take chances.

Georgia laid her hand on the cowling. "Cal, I wish you'd listen to me just once. I've a feeling that—"

Cal Bradley paused in his perusal of the sky and the hundreds of ships lined up on the tarmacs of the great hangars. Puzzled, he looked down.

"Maybe it's silly," she went on, "and I know you'll laugh, but I have a premonition that you're going to crash today."

"The first day of the meet?" True to her prophecy, Cal laughed. "You've just got a case of jitters, honey. I'm going to live through this meet and a good many more. In fact, I'm going to live long enough to buy out your dad and marry you

91

and win a thousand races. Maybe this ship is all I've got in the world, but it's enough. Now, if you don't look out, I'll blast the engine and blow you clean through the grandstand!"

Georgia laughed and backed away, almost bumping into her father, Speed Kyle, who was hobbling up in time to wish Cal luck.

"Be careful!" Georgia called, above the growing roar of the engine.

"Good luck, Cal!" shouted Speed, and with a beaming smile on his weather-beaten face, he watched the small but speedy racing plane taxi away toward the line.

When the dust had settled from Cal's prop wash, Speed turned to his daughter with pretended ferocity. "The idea, telling that youngster to be careful, just when he's out to make the record!"

"He can be careful and fly fast, too, can't he?"

"Humph!" Speed grunted, and took her arm, leading her away toward the grandstand. "There's not so much difference between auto racing and plane racing, Georgia, and there's no difference at all between the fellows that do the driving. Why, as old as I am, I'd give my eye teeth to be up there in one of the Kyle racers giving Cal Bradley the run of his young life."

"You aren't so old, Dad," said Georgia.

"No? Well, I'm the deuce of a lot older than I care to be. I was in the auto racing game in 1902, and I've been building airplanes for fourteen years."

Having heard the story since the days of her hair ribbons, Georgia diverted her attention to the line where three ships were coming in side by side.

"All ready to go," she said. "I hope Cal doesn't turn the pylons too fast."

Speed's grunt was interrupted by the grinding voice through the microphones saying that Cal Bradley, Bill Conklin and Smoke Gregory, the three speed kings of the air, were about to race against each other and the record, and that this was the first of a series of high-speed events which would be held at the National Air Meet.

Speed looked at Conklin's ship with shrewd, appraising eyes. This was Speed's own entry, and though he half-hoped Cal Bradley would win, the flimsy thing of wood and steel which bore the Kyle Aircraft Eagle carried all Speed's hope for immediate glory.

"Wish Bill had some of Cal's fire," he growled. "That ship of mine is twice as good as Cal's. One of these days, Georgia, I'm going to sign up young Bradley and make a star out of him."

"You mean you'd like to have him race for you?"

"Why not? He's the coming bet of the country today, and with him at my sticks, we'd lead the field. I build 'em best, he flies 'em best. Say!" Speed's frown went away under the light of sudden inspiration—"Why don't you persuade him?"

Georgia's glance was meant to be withering, but at that instant the ship flashed across the starting line and captured all of Speed's attention.

Five hundred feet up, Cal Bradley looked to the right and left to assure himself that the other two contestants were regularly spaced out behind him and shot the gun up into its last notch. The three-hundred-horsepower engine chattered and clanked and sent four hundred and forty feet of air behind it in the space of a single second. Three hundred miles an hour, and the air speed indicator was creeping even higher.

It was good to have a live motor in front of him, a sensitive stick in his fingers and a hurtling plane around him. Up ahead there were pylons to turn and wind currents to fight, but they were still ahead. Right now, Cal Bradley was perfectly content to sit in his cockpit and fly.

Directly to the rear, Smoke Gregory was hurling his Jupiter Aircraft ship into Cal's wake. Third in line came Bill Conklin, in the Kyle Eagle. Ahead of them the checkered pyramid which was Pylon One was looming.

Cal settled himself on the cushion his parachute made and prepared for the vertical which would soon be his lot. He spared the briefest glance to the rear to make certain of his airway and saw that Smoke Gregory, in the Jupiter ship, was gaining.

To find out more about *Hurtling Wings* and how you can obtain your copy, go to www.goldenagestories.com.

GLOSSARY

GLOSSARY

STORIES FROM THE GOLDEN AGE *reflect the words and expressions used in the 1930s and 1940s, adding unique flavor and authenticity to the tales. While a character's speech may often reflect regional origins, it also can convey attitudes common in the day. So that readers can better grasp such cultural and historical terms, uncommon words or expressions of the era, the following glossary has been provided.*

---

airdrome: a military air base.

chiselers: people who cheat or swindle.

Columbus: Christopher Columbus (1451–1506), Italian navigator who discovered the New World in the service of Spain while looking for a route to China.

Cosmoline: a substance obtained from the residues of the distillation of petroleum, essentially the same as Vaseline, but of heavy grade. Used as a protective coating for firearms, metals, etc.

cowling: the removable metal housing of an aircraft engine, often designed as part of the airplane's body, containing the cockpit, passenger seating and cargo but excluding the wings.

crate: an airplane.

Curtiss Hawk: US-built fighter aircraft of the 1930s, it was one of the first fighters of the new generation consisting of sleek monoplanes with extensive use of metal in construction and powerful piston engines.

Department of Commerce or **D of C:** the department of the US federal government that promotes and administers domestic and foreign commerce. In 1926, Congress passed an Air Commerce Act that gave the US Department of Commerce some regulation over air facilities, the authority to establish air traffic rules and the authority to issue licenses and certificates.

Floyd Bennett Field: New York City's first municipal airport, now defunct as an active airfield. Located in Brooklyn, it was created by connecting several marsh islands by filling them with pumped sand, and is now physically part of Long Island.

galleons: large three-masted sailing ships, usually with two or more decks; used mainly by the Spanish from the fifteenth to eighteenth centuries for war and commerce.

gangway: a narrow, movable platform or ramp forming a bridge by which to board or leave a ship.

G-men: government men; agents of the Federal Bureau of Investigation.

Gobi: Asia's largest desert, located in China and southern Mongolia.

Graphic: Graflex Speed Graphic camera. It was the dominant portable professional camera from the 1930s through the end of the 1950s.

gyroscopic: having the characteristic of a gyroscope, a device containing a wheel that spins freely within a frame, used on aircraft and ships to help keep them horizontal.

Immelmann: also known as a wingover; an aerial maneuver named after World War I flying ace Max Immelmann. The pilot pulls the aircraft into a vertical climb, then rolls the aircraft back down in the opposite direction. It has become one of the most popular aerial maneuvers in the world.

inertia starter: a device for starting engines. During the energizing of the starter, all movable parts within it are set in motion. After the starter has been fully energized, it is engaged to the crankshaft of the engine and the flywheel energy is transferred to the engine.

Inland Sea: a narrow sea that is 270 miles long, nine to thirty-five miles wide and surrounded by three of Japan's four main islands. Known as *Seto Naikai* or "sea between straits," it is said to be an object of reverence to the Japanese.

JN-9: Curtiss N-9; a seaplane used to train US Navy pilots during World War I. The N-9 was used in 1916 and 1917 for the development of ship-mounted launch catapults and flight testing the new autopilot components intended to be used in pilotless "aerial torpedoes." They were retired by the Navy in 1927.

jury strut: a strut that keeps an aircraft's wings from bowing or snapping when air pressure pushes down on them.

Kanchow: city in southwestern China.

Kawasaki KDA-5: a fighter biplane built by Kawasaki, a Japanese aircraft manufacturer founded in 1918. The first prototype flew in 1932; 380 of these planes were built.

Kobe: a seaport in southern Japan.

line pilot: a pilot that flies a route.

Magellan: Ferdinand Magellan (1480–1521); in 1519 he sailed west around South America and across the Pacific Ocean to the Spice Islands (islands in Indonesia colonized by the Portuguese). He was killed in battle in the Philippines but one of his original five ships, *Victoria*, eventually made it back to Spain. Though Magellan didn't complete the entire circumnavigation, as the expedition's leader he is usually credited with being the first man to circle the globe.

Manchuria: a region of northeast China comprising the modern-day provinces of Heilongjiang, Jilin and Liaoning. It was the homeland of the Manchu people, who conquered China in the seventeenth century, and was hotly contested by the Russians and the Japanese in the late nineteenth and early twentieth centuries. Chinese Communists gained control of the area in 1948.

Morane: French aircraft manufacturer, founded in 1911, which produced monoplane fighter aircraft used in World War I and developed a system to allow machine guns to be mounted on the front of aircraft and fired through the propeller.

NAA: National Aeronautics Association; established in 1922 as a nonprofit organization "dedicated to the advancement of the art, sport and science of aviation in the United States." It is the official record-keeper for US aviation and provides observers and compiles the data necessary to certify aviation and spaceflight records of all kinds.

Nakajima: Japan's first aircraft manufacturer, founded in 1917.

Nationalist government: Chinese Nationalist Party led by Chiang Kai-shek attempting to purge Communism from China and unite the country under one central government. Civil war broke out in 1927 between the Nationalist government and the Red Army led by Mao Tse-tung. China was also involved in intermittent conflicts with Japan since 1931 with full-scale war breaking out in 1937. In 1949 the Nationalist government's power declined and Communist control ensued, forcing the Nationalists from mainland China into Taiwan.

octant: a navigational instrument like the sextant but with an angle of only forty-five degrees.

petcock: a small valve for releasing pressure or for draining a line.

picture hat: a woman's elaborately decorated hat with a very broad brim.

Pinsk: large river port city located in southern Belarus. Pinsk was part of Russia from the late 1700s until 1921, when it became part of Poland. In 1944 it again became part of Russia.

Pizarro: Francisco Pizarro (1471–1541), Spanish conquistador known for conquering Peru's Inca Empire and founding the city of Lima in 1535.

precession: gyroscopic precession; where the axis of a spinning object (i.e., a part of a gyroscope) "wobbles" or has a change in rotational motion when the angular forces made by the aircraft are applied to it. In this case, because the plane is flying on autopilot, changes in direction and changes in the plane's physical location as it flies cause precession in the gyroscope that drives the autopilot, and must therefore be compensated for.

pylons: towers marking turning points in a race among aircraft.

Rising Sun: Japan; the characters that make up Japan's name mean "the sun's origin," which is why Japan is sometimes identified as the "Land of the Rising Sun." It is also the military flag of Japan and was used as the ensign of the Imperial Japanese Navy and the war flag of the Imperial Japanese Army until the end of World War II.

Scheherazade: the female narrator of *The Arabian Nights,* who during one thousand and one adventurous nights saved her life by entertaining her husband, the king, with stories.

Shanghai: city of eastern China at the mouth of the Yangtze River, and the largest city in the country. Shanghai was opened to foreign trade by treaty in 1842 and quickly prospered. France, Great Britain and the United States all held large concessions (rights to use land granted by a government) in the city until the early twentieth century.

shrouds: the ropes connecting the harness and canopy of a parachute.

slipstream: the airstream pushed back by a revolving aircraft propeller.

smacks: any of various small, fully decked, fore-and-aft-rigged vessels used for catching fish or coastal trading.

smear: smash.

struts: supports for a structure such as an aircraft wing, roof or bridge.

tarmac: airport runway.

tide flats: nearly flat coastal areas, alternately covered and exposed by the tides.

tracer: a bullet or shell whose course is made visible by a trail of flames or smoke, used to assist in aiming.

Ural Mountains: a mountain range in what is now the Russian Federation, extending north and south from the Arctic Ocean to near the Caspian Sea, forming a natural boundary between Europe and Asia.

Urga: now Ulan Bator; capital city of Mongolia.

Vasco de Gama: (1469–1524) naval commander whose expedition from Lisbon in 1497 to India led to Portuguese dominance of the Eastern spice trade.

Yellow Sea: an arm of the Pacific Ocean between the Chinese mainland and the Korean Peninsula. It connects with the East China Sea to the south.

L. Ron Hubbard
in the Golden Age
of Pulp Fiction

*In writing an adventure story
a writer has to know that he is adventuring
for a lot of people who cannot.
The writer has to take them here and there
about the globe and show them
excitement and love and realism.
As long as that writer is living the part of an
adventurer when he is hammering
the keys, he is succeeding with his story.*

*Adventuring is a state of mind.
If you adventure through life, you have a
good chance to be a success on paper.*

*Adventure doesn't mean globe-trotting,
exactly, and it doesn't mean great deeds.
Adventuring is like art.
You have to live it to make it real.*

—*L. RON HUBBARD*

L. Ron Hubbard
and American
Pulp Fiction

B ORN March 13, 1911, L. Ron Hubbard lived a life at least as expansive as the stories with which he enthralled a hundred million readers through a fifty-year career.

Originally hailing from Tilden, Nebraska, he spent his formative years in a classically rugged Montana, replete with the cowpunchers, lawmen and desperadoes who would later people his Wild West adventures. And lest anyone imagine those adventures were drawn from vicarious experience, he was not only breaking broncs at a tender age, he was also among the few whites ever admitted into Blackfoot society as a bona fide blood brother. While if only to round out an otherwise rough and tumble youth, his mother was that rarity of her time—a thoroughly educated woman—who introduced her son to the classics of Occidental literature even before his seventh birthday.

But as any dedicated L. Ron Hubbard reader will attest, his world extended far beyond Montana. In point of fact, and as the son of a United States naval officer, by the age of eighteen he had traveled over a quarter of a million miles. Included therein were three Pacific crossings to a then still mysterious Asia, where he ran with the likes of Her British Majesty's agent-in-place

L. Ron Hubbard, left, at Congressional Airport, Washington, DC, 1931, with members of George Washington University flying club.

for North China, and the last in the line of Royal Magicians from the court of Kublai Khan. For the record, L. Ron Hubbard was also among the first Westerners to gain admittance to forbidden Tibetan monasteries below Manchuria, and his photographs of China's Great Wall long graced American geography texts.

Upon his return to the United States and a hasty completion of his interrupted high school education, the young Ron Hubbard entered George Washington University. There, as fans of his aerial adventures may have heard, he earned his wings as a pioneering barnstormer at the dawn of American aviation. He also earned a place in free-flight record books for the longest sustained flight above Chicago. Moreover, as a roving reporter for *Sportsman Pilot* (featuring his first professionally penned articles), he further helped inspire a generation of pilots who would take America to world airpower.

Immediately beyond his sophomore year, Ron embarked on the first of his famed ethnological expeditions, initially to then untrammeled Caribbean shores (descriptions of which would later fill a whole series of West Indies mystery-thrillers). That the Puerto Rican interior would also figure into the future of Ron Hubbard stories was likewise no accident. For in addition to cultural studies of the island, a 1932–33

LRH expedition is rightly remembered as conducting the first complete mineralogical survey of a Puerto Rico under United States jurisdiction.

There was many another adventure along this vein: As a lifetime member of the famed Explorers Club, L. Ron Hubbard charted North Pacific waters with the first shipboard radio direction finder, and so pioneered a long-range navigation system universally employed until the late twentieth century. While not to put too fine an edge on it, he also held a rare Master Mariner's license to pilot any vessel, of any tonnage in any ocean.

Yet lest we stray too far afield, there is an LRH note at this juncture in his saga, and it reads in part:

"I started out writing for the pulps, writing the best I knew, writing for every mag on the stands, slanting as well as I could."

To which one might add: His earliest submissions date from the summer of 1934, and included tales drawn from true-to-life Asian adventures, with characters roughly modeled on British/American intelligence operatives he had known in Shanghai. His early Westerns were similarly peppered with details drawn from personal experience. Although therein lay a first hard lesson from the often cruel world of the pulps. His first Westerns were soundly rejected as lacking the authenticity of a Max Brand yarn

Capt. L. Ron Hubbard in Ketchikan, Alaska, 1940, on his Alaskan Radio Experimental Expedition, the first of three voyages conducted under the Explorers Club flag.

(a particularly frustrating comment given L. Ron Hubbard's Westerns came straight from his Montana homeland, while Max Brand was a mediocre New York poet named Frederick Schiller Faust, who turned out implausible six-shooter tales from the terrace of an Italian villa).

Nevertheless, and needless to say, L. Ron Hubbard persevered and soon earned a reputation as among the most publishable names in pulp fiction, with a ninety percent placement rate of first-draft manuscripts. He was also among the most prolific, averaging between seventy and a hundred thousand words a month. Hence the rumors that L. Ron Hubbard had redesigned a typewriter for faster keyboard action and pounded out manuscripts on a continuous roll of butcher paper to save the precious seconds it took to insert a single sheet of paper into manual typewriters of the day.

That all L. Ron Hubbard stories did not run beneath said byline is yet another aspect of pulp fiction lore. That is, as publishers periodically rejected manuscripts from top-drawer authors if only to avoid paying top dollar, L. Ron Hubbard and company just as frequently replied with submissions under various pseudonyms. In Ron's case, the

A Man of Many Names

Between 1934 and 1950, L. Ron Hubbard authored more than fifteen million words of fiction in more than two hundred classic publications. To supply his fans and editors with stories across an array of genres and pulp titles, he adopted fifteen pseudonyms in addition to his already renowned L. Ron Hubbard byline.

Winchester Remington Colt
Lt. Jonathan Daly
Capt. Charles Gordon
Capt. L. Ron Hubbard
Bernard Hubbel
Michael Keith
Rene Lafayette
Legionnaire 148
Legionnaire 14830
Ken Martin
Scott Morgan
Lt. Scott Morgan
Kurt von Rachen
Barry Randolph
Capt. Humbert Reynolds

list included: Rene Lafayette,
Captain Charles Gordon, Lt. Scott
Morgan and the notorious Kurt von
Rachen—supposedly on the lam
for a murder rap, while hammering
out two-fisted prose in Argentina.
The point: While L. Ron Hubbard
as Ken Martin spun stories of
Southeast Asian intrigue, LRH as
Barry Randolph authored tales of

romance on the Western range—which, stretching
between a dozen genres is how he came to stand
among the two hundred elite authors providing close
to a million tales through the glory days of American
Pulp Fiction.

*L. Ron Hubbard,
circa 1930, at the
outset of a literary
career that would
finally span half
a century.*

In evidence of exactly that, by 1936 L. Ron Hubbard
was literally leading pulp fiction's elite as president of New
York's American Fiction Guild. Members included a veritable
pulp hall of fame: Lester "Doc Savage" Dent, Walter "The
Shadow" Gibson, and the legendary Dashiell Hammett—to
cite but a few.

Also in evidence of just where L. Ron Hubbard stood
within his first two years on the American pulp circuit: By the
spring of 1937, he was ensconced in Hollywood, adopting a
Caribbean thriller for Columbia Pictures, remembered today as
The Secret of Treasure Island. Comprising fifteen thirty-minute
episodes, the L. Ron Hubbard screenplay led to the most
profitable matinée serial in Hollywood history. In accord with
Hollywood culture, he was thereafter continually called upon

The 1937 Secret of Treasure Island, *a fifteen-episode serial adapted for the screen by L. Ron Hubbard from his novel,* Murder at Pirate Castle.

to rewrite/doctor scripts—most famously for long-time friend and fellow adventurer Clark Gable.

In the interim—and herein lies another distinctive chapter of the L. Ron Hubbard story—he continually worked to open Pulp Kingdom gates to up-and-coming authors. Or, for that matter, anyone who wished to write. It was a fairly unconventional stance, as markets were already thin and competition razor sharp. But the fact remains, it was an L. Ron Hubbard hallmark that he vehemently lobbied on behalf of young authors—regularly supplying instructional articles to trade journals, guest-lecturing to short story classes at George Washington University and Harvard, and even founding his own creative writing competition. It was established in 1940, dubbed the Golden Pen, and guaranteed winners both New York representation and publication in *Argosy*.

But it was John W. Campbell Jr.'s *Astounding Science Fiction* that finally proved the most memorable LRH vehicle. While every fan of L. Ron Hubbard's galactic epics undoubtedly knows the story, it nonetheless bears repeating: By late 1938, the pulp publishing magnate of Street & Smith was determined to revamp *Astounding Science Fiction* for broader readership. In particular, senior editorial director F. Orlin Tremaine called for stories with a stronger *human element*. When acting editor John W. Campbell balked, preferring his spaceship-driven

112

tales, Tremaine enlisted Hubbard. Hubbard, in turn, replied with the genre's first truly *character-driven* works, wherein heroes are pitted not against bug-eyed monsters but the mystery and majesty of deep space itself—and thus was launched the Golden Age of Science Fiction.

The names alone are enough to quicken the pulse of any science fiction aficionado, including LRH friend and protégé, Robert Heinlein, Isaac Asimov, A. E. van Vogt and Ray Bradbury. Moreover, when coupled with LRH stories of fantasy, we further come to what's rightly been described as the foundation of every modern tale of horror: L. Ron Hubbard's immortal *Fear.* It was rightly proclaimed by Stephen King as one of the very few works to genuinely warrant that overworked term "classic"—as in: *"This is a classic tale of creeping, surreal menace and horror. . . . This is one of the really, really good ones."*

To accommodate the greater body of L. Ron Hubbard fantasies, Street & Smith inaugurated *Unknown*—a classic pulp if there ever was one, and wherein readers were soon thrilling to the likes of *Typewriter in the Sky* and *Slaves of Sleep* of which Frederik Pohl would declare: *"There are bits and pieces from Ron's work that became part of the language in ways that very few other writers managed."*

And, indeed, at J. W. Campbell Jr.'s insistence, Ron was regularly drawing on themes from the Arabian Nights and

L. Ron Hubbard, 1948, among fellow science fiction luminaries at the World Science Fiction Convention in Toronto.

so introducing readers to a world of genies, jinn, Aladdin and Sinbad—all of which, of course, continue to float through cultural mythology to this day.

At least as influential in terms of post-apocalypse stories was L. Ron Hubbard's 1940 *Final Blackout*. Generally acclaimed as the finest anti-war novel of the decade and among the ten best works of the genre ever authored—here, too, was a tale that would live on in ways few other writers imagined.

Portland, Oregon, 1943; L. Ron Hubbard, captain of the US Navy subchaser PC 815.

Hence, the later Robert Heinlein verdict: "Final Blackout *is as perfect a piece of science fiction as has ever been written.*"

Like many another who both lived and wrote American pulp adventure, the war proved a tragic end to Ron's sojourn in the pulps. He served with distinction in four theaters and was highly decorated for commanding corvettes in the North Pacific. He was also grievously wounded in combat, lost many a close friend and colleague and thus resolved to say farewell to pulp fiction and devote himself to what it had supported these many years—namely, his serious research.

But in no way was the LRH literary saga at an end, for as he wrote some thirty years later, in 1980:

"Recently there came a period when I had little to do. This was novel in a life so crammed with busy years, and I decided to amuse myself by writing a novel that was pure *science fiction."*

That work was *Battlefield Earth: A Saga of the Year 3000*. It was an immediate *New York Times* bestseller and, in fact, the first international science fiction blockbuster in decades. It was, however, not L. Ron Hubbard's magnum opus, as that distinction is generally reserved for his next and final work: The 1.2 million word *Mission Earth*.

> **Final Blackout**
> *is as perfect*
> *a piece of*
> *science fiction*
> *as has ever*
> *been written.*
>
> —Robert Heinlein

How he managed those 1.2 million words in just over twelve months is yet another piece of the L. Ron Hubbard legend. But the fact remains, he did indeed author a ten-volume *dekalogy* that lives in publishing history for the fact that each and every volume of the series was also a *New York Times* bestseller.

Moreover, as subsequent generations discovered L. Ron Hubbard through republished works and novelizations of his screenplays, the mere fact of his name on a cover signaled an international bestseller. . . . Until, to date, sales of his works exceed hundreds of millions, and he otherwise remains among the most enduring and widely read authors in literary history. Although as a final word on the tales of L. Ron Hubbard, perhaps it's enough to simply reiterate what editors told readers in the glory days of American Pulp Fiction:

He writes the way he does, brothers, because he's been there, seen it and done it!

THE STORIES FROM THE GOLDEN AGE

Your ticket to adventure starts here with the Stories from
the Golden Age collection by master storyteller L. Ron Hubbard.
These gripping tales are set in a kaleidoscope of exotic locales and brim
with fascinating characters, including some of the
most vile villains, dangerous dames and brazen heroes
you'll ever get to meet.

The entire collection of over one hundred and fifty stories is being
released in a series of eighty books and audiobooks.
For an up-to-date listing of available titles,
go to www.goldenagestories.com.

AIR ADVENTURE

Arctic Wings	*Man-Killers of the Air*
The Battling Pilot	*On Blazing Wings*
Boomerang Bomber	*Red Death Over China*
The Crate Killer	*Sabotage in the Sky*
The Dive Bomber	*Sky Birds Dare!*
Forbidden Gold	*The Sky-Crasher*
Hurtling Wings	*Trouble on His Wings*
The Lieutenant Takes the Sky	*Wings Over Ethiopia*

FAR-FLUNG ADVENTURE

SEA ADVENTURE

TALES FROM THE ORIENT

The Devil—With Wings *Pearl Pirate*
The Falcon Killer *The Red Dragon*
Five Mex for a Million *Spy Killer*
Golden Hell *Tah*
The Green God *The Trail of the Red Diamonds*
Hurricane's Roar *Wind-Gone-Mad*
Inky Odds *Yellow Loot*
Orders Is Orders

MYSTERY

The Blow Torch Murder *The Grease Spot*
Brass Keys to Murder *Killer Ape*
Calling Squad Cars! *Killer's Law*
The Carnival of Death *The Mad Dog Murder*
The Chee-Chalker *Mouthpiece*
Dead Men Kill *Murder Afloat*
The Death Flyer *The Slickers*
Flame City *They Killed Him Dead*

FANTASY

SCIENCE FICTION

WESTERN

The Baron of Coyote River	*Man for Breakfast*
Blood on His Spurs	*The No-Gun Gunhawk*
Boss of the Lazy B	*The No-Gun Man*
Branded Outlaw	*The Ranch That No One Would Buy*
Cattle King for a Day	*Reign of the Gila Monster*
Come and Get It	*Ride 'Em, Cowboy*
Death Waits at Sundown	*Ruin at Rio Piedras*
Devil's Manhunt	*Shadows from Boot Hill*
The Ghost Town Gun-Ghost	*Silent Pards*
Gun Boss of Tumbleweed	*Six-Gun Caballero*
Gunman!	*Stacked Bullets*
Gunman's Tally	*Stranger in Town*
The Gunner from Gehenna	*Tinhorn's Daughter*
Hoss Tamer	*The Toughest Ranger*
Johnny, the Town Tamer	*Under the Diehard Brand*
King of the Gunmen	*Vengeance Is Mine!*
The Magic Quirt	*When Gilhooly Was in Flower*